My Highland Raider

Miriam Minger

All rights reserved.

No part of this publication may be sold, copied, distributed, reproduced or transmitted in any form or by any means, mechanical or digital, including photocopying and recording or by any information storage and retrieval system without the prior written permission of both the publisher, Oliver Heber Books and the author, Miriam Minger, except in the case of brief quotations embodied in critical articles and reviews.

PUBLISHER'S NOTE: This is a work of fiction. Names, characters, places, and incidents either are the product of the author's imagination or are used fictitiously. Any resemblance to actual persons, living or dead, business establishments, events, or locales is entirely coincidental.

COPYRIGHT © Miriam Minger

Published by Oliver-Heber Books

0 9 8 7 6 5 4 3 2 1

1

NEAR THE CAMPBELL STRONGHOLD,
ARGYLLSHIRE, SCOTLAND, 1307

"*I canna marry you, Gavin, I've agreed tae wed another. For clan and honor... you must try tae understand, but I will always love you. Dinna forget me...*"

Forget her? Even now as he stood aboard his ship anchored in a secluded cove, the memory of Cora's last words to him a year ago pierced Gavin MacLachlan's heart like the sharpest blade, his fists clenching in fury.

At Clan Campbell, aye, for he blamed them for forcing the woman he loved into a marriage she hadn't wanted... no matter she had spoken of clan and honor.

He had seen the tears glistening in her beautiful sea blue eyes.

He had felt her shaking in his arms before she had pushed herself away from him and fled from the stronghold chapel where they had met in secret for months.

A formidable stronghold in northern Argyll that housed not only Cora and her parents but Rory, the chieftain of Clan Campbell, as well as his family and nearest relations—uncles and aunts and cousins and all those that supported them.

Serving men and women, cooks, stable hands, armorers and countless others, along with the warriors who guarded the palisade surrounding the stout structures of the large village within those towering log walls.

Gavin had ultimately become one of those warriors, having come north with his mother years earlier after the untimely death of his father, a farrier. Before that wretched event, they had lived near MacLachlan Castle among his father's kinsmen, but his mother, a seamstress, had wanted to move closer to her people that served the chieftain of Clan Campbell.

Gavin had been fourteen when he apprenticed with a crusty old fisherman and learned not only the best fishing grounds along the rugged coast of Argyll, but the mysteries of wind and currents and weather, from the calmest sea to the wildest tempest.

By nineteen, he had grown taller and broader of shoulder than other young men his age and so strong that by the time he was twenty, he had begun driving an oxcart loaded with the early morning's catch in heavy barrels, to the stronghold.

Aye, he was a man of humble beginnings, which had doomed him and Cora from the start.

She, a cousin of Rory Campbell and of such stunning beauty with her raven-black hair and milk-white skin to make men's knees weak at the sight of her. Just as his knees had grown weak when he spied her for the first time.

She had come to the stronghold market with a well-dressed woman he learned later was her mother, and had paused at the fish stall moments after he arrived with a fresh cartload.

He had been up since before dawn and no doubt smelled of that morning's catch, which to him was a fine, clean scent of wind and salt spray.

His clothes damp with sweat and sticking to his body, his shoulder-length, dark red hair tied back with a strip of leather to keep it out of his face.

He had been so focused upon his task of unloading the cart that he didn't even look up until he heard the softest feminine laughter, Gavin meeting the eyes of the loveliest lass he had ever seen.

The kindly woman who stood beside her had laughed, too, both of them pointing to the herring that had caught itself in his belt, its silvery tail flapping.

Gavin could have felt embarrassed, but instead he had merely shrugged and laughed with them, and pulled out the fish and offered it with a flourish to Cora.

Cora Campbell.

He had learned her name later, too, and of her high rank at the stronghold as the chieftain's first cousin, but it wasn't chafing at his own lesser status that had made Gavin decide then and there to become a warrior.

He had wanted to be closer to her... and living the life of a fisherman would only keep him out at sea but for his twice weekly trips to the stronghold.

Even earning the nickname of "Trout" from his fellow warriors didn't deter him. Within five months, Gavin's strapping size and impressive skill with the sword had earned him a promotion from manning the palisade to a guard in the chieftain's hall.

Gavin had lived and breathed to see her, which

was often enough when Rory's closest family members gathered together for meals.

Her furtive glances in his direction making his heart pound... the delicate pink blush of her cheeks making him certain that her heart raced, too.

So it continued for weeks, his frustration growing that they had not found a chance to speak to each other—until one day, as if by a miracle, her lady's maid sought him out near the barracks with a message.

"The chapel at noon... meet my mistress there."

If he had thought his heart pounded before, nothing could have prepared him for the emotion of finally seeing Cora face-to-face and alone, but for her maid waiting a discreet distance away.

Cora's gaze darting from the chapel entrance, as if she feared at any moment they might be discovered, and back to his face, half cloaked in shadow from where they stood together near a side altar.

The air tinged with the pungent smell of incense and something else, aye, the heady scent of damask roses.

The memory of her perfume was so vivid that Gavin felt as if it were yesterday, making him pound his clenched fist against the ship railing.

The memory of her soft lips pressed to his in the sweetest first kiss, filling him with such longing that he could scarcely breathe.

A kiss made all too brief when they had been startled apart by a priest appearing at the front altar—God forgive him, Gavin could have throttled the man. Cora had fled toward the entrance while he had waited in the shadows until he felt it was safe to leave unnoticed.

So they had managed to see each other on nearly a

dozen occasions over the next few months, each meeting more precious than the one before. Yet the last time she came to him, something had changed.

Cora had seemed tenuous and fearful, her slender body tense when he had taken her in his arms and whispered against the delicate curve of her ear.

"Marry me, Cora. Be my bride."

Her refusal had come swiftly... too swiftly, as if she had sensed beforehand what he intended to say. Then her tears, her trembling, and she was gone from him.

His arms empty and her words echoing like a death knell in his brain.

He had left the chapel after their final meeting believing that he would never see Cora again.

His heart filled with hatred for the Campbells.

Hatred for those that he believed had forced her into acquiescing to a marriage to Earl Seoras MacDougall, a man known to be as ruthless as he was rich and powerful.

No, it couldn't have been simply for clan and honor that Cora had become another man's bride. Some coercion and treachery had to have been afoot... for as soon as Gavin had headed for the barracks, a host of his fellow warriors, grim-faced, had flanked him with their weapons drawn and escorted him instead to the stronghold gates.

The one he had thought to be a friend, Blair Campbell, hissing in his ear.

"Did you think no one would ever notice what you've been about, man? What have you tae offer the chieftain's own cousin? Nothing! She's pledged tae wed another, a powerful alliance for our clan—and not the likes of you, Trout. Find yourself a fisherman's daughter tae keep you warm and dinna ever come back if you want tae live."

The man's words the bitterest of memories, Gavin had to restrain himself from roaring out a blistering curse that would have been heard at the Campbell stronghold only a league away.

Dinna ever come back—but he was back.

Not a humble fisherman, but a fearsome raider who had made himself known far and wide in the span of one year.

A year spent in relentless forays along the English coast and as far south as Normandy, an iron-banded chest below deck filled with more gold than any Highland laird or chieftain had ever seen. Two more chests had been buried on a small island ten leagues off the coast of Argyll—one of them just the other day on his way north. A remote, windswept place he had discovered during his fishing days, and where he would go if he ever needed to seek refuge.

He had become rich beyond measure, but the spoils gotten by attacking most ships he and his men came across had left nothing but the bitter taste of ashes in his mouth.

Cora was forever lost to him, or so he had believed until a week ago.

After spending the summer months plying the waters near Normandy, he had sailed back to Scotland and docked his ship near Dumfries, far to the south to trade his plunder for coin, and had heard incredible news.

Heart-stopping news.

Cora's husband, Earl Seoras, had been slain by Gavin's own cousin Gabriel MacLachlan.

Cora was married no longer, but a widow. . . the unexpected revelation spurring Gavin northward to find her.

Aye, before those hated Campbells could marry

her off again. He hadn't known anywhere else to look but with her parents, Owen and Glenis Campbell, for surely Cora hadn't remained at the fortress given over for another to rule.

Only an unexpected stop along the way to save the wife and young son of a childhood friend, Conall Campbell, had slowed him down, Gavin's wealth increased by the sultan's jewels that he had earned for his trouble.

Och, *half* of the jewels—the rest shared with Conall as a wedding present. The black-haired Highlander and his elder brother Cameron had saved his life long ago... two Campbells that Gavin didn't begrudge the air they breathed.

Yet as for the rest of their clan, they would taste his wrath as soon as he found Cora and carried her safely away. He had riches enough to enlist an army of warriors to help him enact his plan for vengeance... but for now, he needed stealth to find her.

Stealth and a good dose of luck, for the Campbell stronghold was near impregnable. Gavin had learned as much while a guard there—

"Laird, will we remain in this cove another night?" came his helmsman's voice jarring into his grim thoughts. "Surely our presence will be discovered if we linger too long—"

"This mist willna lift for a good while yet, so stop fretting like a nursemaid," Gavin cut him off, the wiry Scotsman standing barely above his elbow.

Brody MacCreary had been with him the longest of the thirty sailors aboard his ship, all of them made eager to join up with Gavin at the prospect of sharing equally in the spoils of their raids. Aye, a dangerous life but a better one than they had known, some of them failed farmers or disenchanted soldiers and others simply down on their luck with no steady work to be found.

Gavin had earned their fierce loyalty by fair treatment and the opportunity to wreak havoc against the English that had tormented Scotland for as long as any of them could remember—and now they awaited his orders for whatever he had planned for the Campbells.

Yet he would not risk their lives for what he considered a personal mission, and it was wiser that he set out alone. One man would elicit no immediate alarm, but a half dozen or more would draw his enemies' attention like flies to fresh dung. Better that they remain ready and aboard ship for when he returned with Cora—och, God, was it possible that she would be safe within his arms by morning?

If he found her, Gavin reminded himself grimly as he glanced at Brody, who stood silently beside him.

The helmsman stared into the swirling mist that seemed to have grown thicker with each passing moment, and drew his black woolen cloak more tightly around him. Gavin did the same, his cloak as black but with a hood that he settled over his head.

It seemed any traces of summer had faded the further north they sailed, the air cooler, the sky darker, the clouds heavier. No rain yet, but moisture dripped from the dense canopy of leaves above them and plunked down upon the canvas drawn over the middle section of the ship where his men had taken cover from the elements. Even the birds were silent and nestled beneath their wings at the dreariness of the day, but to Gavin, the weather was a blessing.

So, too, would the Campbells be nestled in their homes in front of their hearth fires, though he had no doubt there would be guards aplenty manning the palisade and front gates. Yet the procuring of supplies and foodstuffs must continue no matter the sodden weather, and the market would be open for business, just as it had been when Gavin had delivered fresh fish to the stronghold.

It seemed so long ago that the future had appeared as brilliant as the sun with Cora sweetly declaring her love for him at their every meeting, only to have her torn from his side to satisfy Clan Campbell's lust for power. He was twenty-two now, but felt so much older.

. .

"So you'll go through with this madness even though you dinna know if the lass is among her people or no," Brody said under his breath as if already anticipating Gavin's answer.

"Aye. Her parents' home lies around the corner from the market—so it willna take me but a few strides tae reach their door. If she's there, God willing, I'll have her hiding with me in an oxcart in a blink."

"If she agrees tae go with you, Laird. People change with time—and who can say what the lass suffered while wed tae Earl Seoras? I was with you at that Dumfries inn when we learned the bastard had been slain, remember? It's an evil man that falls victim to his own warrior's sword, aye, and the world is well rid of him. There may be no marks upon her skin, but in her mind, her heart? Och, I wouldna be surprised if she doesna wish for a man tae touch her ever again—"

"By God, Brody, enough!" Gavin clamped his mouth shut in fury at his outburst, but thankfully the mist was so dense now that his words were sucked up as if they had never been spoken. "Time tae go, night is falling. Dinna forget my instructions. If I dinna return by midmorning, take the ship into deep water and wait for my signal—but for no more than a day. If

I've not been captured... or worse, I'll light a fire along the beach. If you see nothing from me within that time, then Godspeed tae the lot of you."

"Aye, Laird... though you're more a lovesick fool than the infamous devil of the seas tae steal into a stronghold with such odds against you. Godspeed!"

Devil of the seas. So that name had spread far and wide from the throats of the men whose lives he'd spared, though he had ransacked their ships and burned many a vessel to ashes upon the waves.

A furious, head-spinning year that would have turned into another, and another, if he hadn't heard that the woman he loved had become a widow.

A widow... and soon to be his bride. He had only to find Cora, God help him, his plan to hide outside the stronghold until first light when the great gates would be opened to the oxcarts and horse-drawn wagons heading to market.

Gavin hitching a ride in one of them.

He said no more to Brody, but climbed over the railing near the prow and jumped onto the rocky beach.

Some of his men had clambered out from under the canvas to stand alongside the helmsman in the gathering dusk, Gavin giving them a last nod before he clutched the hilt of his sword and lunged into the trees.

2

THE CAMPBELL STRONGHOLD, ARGYLLSHIRE, SCOTLAND

"**D**aughter, you must wake. Cora. . . please, we've so little time. You must wake!"

Cora Campbell rolled over in bed, so muddled from sleep that she felt as if she had been drugged. She stared up in confusion at her mother, Glenis, who shook her roughly by the shoulder as if desperate to rouse her.

"My dearest child, how can I help you if you willna heed me? Ah, God, tae be born a woman with beauty and rank is the devil's curse!"

Cora blinked at the vehemence in her mother's voice, usually so kindly, which made her sit up as if she'd been doused with icy water and throw back the covers. "Mama, what has happened?"

"Word came late last night from the clan council that a husband has been chosen for you—but I willna stand for it! Not again after all you've suffered."

"A-a husband?" Cora didn't need her mother grabbing at her arm to jump out of bed and stand shivering in the dimly lit room, but not from the cool air. As her mother nodded and ran to throw open the chest at the foot of the bed, Cora hastened to her side, her heart pounding.

Why had she ever thought that coming home would prove a refuge for her? What madness had overcome her to believe her clan would grant her ample time to heal from the nightmare of her marriage to Seoras before any talk of another one? She had been at the stronghold for only two months.

"Here, quickly, you must dress. It's been all I could do tae let you rest as long as possible, but there was nothing tae be done at night. Now, though, the market will soon be open—"

"Mama, you speak in riddles!" Racked again by confusion, Cora nonetheless hastily stripped out of her linen nightgown and tossed it onto the bed. "Why do you speak of the market?"

"It's your only chance, Cora—here, wear this one."

Cora obliged her and pulled a woolen gown of dark blue over her head even as her mother began to weep softly.

"Men and their plans. . . their alliances, their thirst for power while it's the women that are made tae suffer. If only I'd known what had happened tae make you a widow before you returned home tae us, Cora. I would have told you tae take refuge instead at a convent—ah, God, I pray that it's not too late! Here, bind up your hair beneath this serving maid's cap."

Her hands shaking at her mother's distress, Cora wound her long tresses into a tight knot and thrust the blue linen cap over her head and pulled it down over her ears. Next came a black cloak lined with warm fur that she threw around her shoulders, her feet shod last in sturdy leather slippers.

If her heart had pounded before, now Cora felt as if her pulse couldn't race any faster as her mother grabbed her hand and pulled her toward the door to her bedchamber.

"Your father and I are of the same mind and wish you tae flee this place! It's a northern laird they wish you tae wed—a much older man and as eager for this alliance tae strengthen his own power among the Highland clans. Not a thing of love at all and you so deserve love, Cora. . . even if it's holy vows that you take as a bride of the Church. Come!"

Now Cora felt tears sting her eyes and nearly blind her as she followed her mother out into the main room of their home.

You so deserve love, Cora. Her heart ached as memories assailed her. . . painful memories she had tried so hard to forget.

Why think of the past at all when the man she loved had drowned at sea? So a message bearing the unhappy news had come to her a week after she wed Seoras MacDougall—when she had only agreed to the marriage to save Gavin MacLachlan's life!

She should have known that someone would one day notice her slipping away to the chapel to meet him, Cora trembling now at the memory of his arms around her.

The strength of him.

The warmth of him.

His breath against her cheek when he had bent his head to press his lips to hers, Cora's fingers entwining in his dark red hair.

She had teased him about the length of it, falling below his shoulders though he usually had it tied back with a leather strip.

The first time she'd seen him at the fish stall, standing so tall and strong, had made her heart leap against her breast.

His offer of a wriggling herring making her laugh until his handsome grin had made her breath seem to stop.

She had fallen in love with him from that very moment... and when her clansmen had threatened to kill him if she did not agree to marry Earl Seoras, she had gone to meet Gavin that one last time, feeling as if the world had ceased spinning, the sun gone dim.

The light fading in his penetrating brown eyes when she had refused his offer of marriage, cutting her so deeply that she had fled from the chapel... never to see him again.

Aye, she had known love as wondrous as what she'd seen between Magdalene and her strapping husband, Gabriel MacLachlan, when they had arrived at the MacDougall fortress—now commanded by her cousin Cameron Campbell—the same day that Seoras had been slain.

Cora had said then that she hoped one day she would know love like Magdalene knew love, a desperate wish that Gavin might still be alive and somehow she would find herself free of Seoras.

At least one part had come true, her cruel husband cut down by Gabriel's sword that very night. Yet even if Gavin still lived, her clansmen had sworn to kill him if he ever came near her again—

"Daughter, embrace me and then you must go," Owen Campbell said grimly from the front entranceway where Cora's mother had led her. She nearly crumpled at the tears in her father's eyes while her mother had begun to sob. Both of them gray-haired now and aged more than their years at the sorrow they had suffered, too, over the unwanted marriage forced upon her.

Cora fell into her father's arms and kissed his

damp cheek even as he pressed into her hand a small leather bag that was heavy with coins.

"Dinna tell us where you're bound, Cora, just go. You swore when you returned that you would never marry again for clan or honor, and we're helping you keep that vow. I canna bear tae see you so wretched and unhappy again."

"Oh, Papa!" Cora cried out, but he shook his head and pushed her gently away from him to look sternly into her eyes.

"Your clansmen are certain tae try and find you, for you've a great value tae them—damn them all! My own kin, but I curse the way you've been treated and willna stand for it, the same as your mother. I will send a messenger as soon as I can tae King Robert at Dumbarton Castle tae intervene on your behalf and spare you from this marriage, so seek him out in three weeks' time, do you understand me?"

"Aye," Cora murmured, a glimmer of hope flaring though she wondered if the king would truly thwart her kinsmen's intention to marry her off again. Clan Campbell had sworn allegiance to him only two months ago after countless years under their MacDougall overlords, their loyalty still being tested. "I will do as you say."

"Go, then, as quickly as you can tae the market and hide yourself in a wagon. You'll be free of the stronghold soon enough. Find the nearest farm and purchase a good, sound horse and then ride from north Argyll as fast as you can. Be wary, though, and stay well off the road when you stop tae rest. Your mother has a bag of food for you, oatcakes and salted venison. A hunk of cheese. It should be enough until you reach a convent—och, lass, forget you heard me say it."

Cora nodded as her mother pressed the bag into

her hand, gave her a kiss, and then the two of them together hustled her to the door. She had only a moment to glance over her shoulder at the home she'd known since childhood, and then she was standing outside, her head fairly spinning.

She could hear her mother weeping through the heavy door closed behind her, and the husky murmurs of her father trying to comfort her, which made Cora's eyes fill again with tears.

Useless tears! They were risking much to encourage her to flee and she wouldn't waste the chance they had given her. She pulled the hood of her cloak over her cap and glanced to her right and left.

The narrow street in front of her parents' home was empty and quiet, but Cora could hear life stirring around her as men, women, and children awoke to another day.

A cool, dank day with the night's mist still swirling and thick around her as a rooster crowed nearby, and then another, announcing the dawn. She could hear horses nickering and the low groan of oxen pulling their heavy loads into the market and the creaking of wagon wheels, which told her that the stronghold gates had been opened wide to merchants and artisans come to sell their wares.

That made her think again of Gavin at his fish stall and his smile that had stilled her breath, but she shoved away the haunting memory.

When she had first seen him in August two years ago, she had only been seventeen... and now she was nineteen and felt as if she had lived a lifetime of unhappiness and sorrow.

Mayhap the life of a nun would give her some peace, aye, she could pray that it be so. God keep her that she find her way safely to a convent...

Ducking her head as she set out toward the market, Cora remembered then that Magdalene, Seoras's younger sister, had spent four years feigning madness at the Carmelite order near Dumbarton. That wouldn't be far at all from the castle where her father had bade her to seek out King Robert, fresh hope burning brighter inside her that all might yet be well.

She would throw herself at his feet and beg him to spare her more unhappiness, Cora so intent upon her thoughts that she didn't see the oxcart rumbling out of the mist toward the market until it was almost too late.

Gasping, she jumped aside and nearly careened with a great hulking shape that had appeared as if out of nowhere, a strong hand grabbing her elbow to pull her further out of harm's way.

Somehow she had the presence of mind to duck her head again before her rescuer could see her face, aye, for it had to be a man with such a height and breadth of shoulder—ah, God, one of the stronghold guards in a swirling black cloak?

Her heart thundered as the man released her and disappeared into the mist in the direction Cora had come from, while she hurried onward. Within a few steps more, she was deep into the heart of the market that had erupted into noise and commotion as stalls were loaded with goods from the oxcarts and wagons.

She had to sidestep again to stay out of the way, her gaze darting furtively from beneath her hood to find one that was already empty and mayhap ready to leave the market. Her heartbeat sounded like a drum in her ears, she had grown so anxious to find a place to hide as the morning sky was beginning to brighten and the mist was receding.

"Och, lass, watch your step for the ox dung!" shouted a merchant, Cora nodding nervously and rushing toward the stalls set up against the white stucco wall of the chapel.

The chapel where she had broken Gavin's heart—and her own. Another merchant appeared to be haggling with a farmer whose wagon had been emptied, the two men facing away from her as she crept forward and climbed into the back.

Her hands shaking so badly that she feared they would hear her burrowing beneath a canvas, the wagon bed damp beneath her and smelling of dirt and turnips.

"Is this all you brought me tae sell, man?" demanded one of the men in a gruff voice, clearly indignant, as Cora closed her eyes tight and prayed that she wouldn't be found.

"What do you mean? You'll be selling this fine load for twice the price we agreed upon, so why are you complaining? Now give me what you owe me and I'll be on my way. My wife will beat me round the head with a spoon if I come home with less than she's expecting."

To Cora's surprise, the disgruntled merchant slapped his hand against the side of the wagon where she had laid her head. A gasp escaped her, but fortunately the sound was drowned out by a great bellow from an ox as she clamped her hand over her mouth.

Her eyes wide.

Her heart in her throat.

Fear gripping her that at any moment the canvas would be thrown back and she would be discovered.

Still the men argued until they came to an agreement, with the chinking sound of coins changing hands, and then the farmer climbed onto the wagon and snapped the reins. With a jerk, the wagon creaked into motion and not a slow pace, either, the farmer clearly eager to be on his way.

It was dark beneath the canvas, but Cora managed to stuff her coin bag into the bigger one filled with food and shove it into a corner near her head. Then she drew up her legs and hugged her knees, bracing them against the side for there was nothing else to hold onto as the wagon rumbled toward what she hoped was the entrance to the stronghold.

Was it to be so simple, then? Thank God, thank God! She held her breath, anxious and yet daring to feel relieved until she felt a slight dip as if someone had climbed onto the wagon.

A quick movement and almost imperceptible for how swiftly it happened, except for the canvas lifting and then settling back over Cora as a steely arm went round her waist.

"Dinna make a sound!" hissed a masculine voice in the darkness while all she wanted to do was scream, her face burning with alarm.

A steely arm that hugged her tighter, her back against her captor's chest, his huge hand covering her mouth at the sound of guards bidding farewell to the farmer as the wagon rumbled through the gates.

3

"Shh, lass, no harm will come tae us if you lie still."

Lie still? Cora couldn't move a muscle for how closely her captor held her, his warm breath fanning the back of her neck and giving her chills.

She felt sick and terrified all rolled into one, her stomach roiling with every jarring bump in the road that led away from the stronghold.

No one had held her thusly since Seoras, and his attentions had never been gentle or kind but brusque and brutal. Besieged by memories, Cora truly thought she would retch and had to swallow back bile burning at the base of her throat.

This stranger holding her made her realize just how much she now abhorred the touch of a man, and she thought to sink her teeth into his fingers to make him remove his hand from her mouth.

She couldn't breathe! Seoras had done that to her, too, covering her mouth so no one would hear her pleas for him to release her as agonized tears burned her eyes. His attentions had been bestial, degrading, and had made her hate him more than she thought she could hate anyone— until one night she had blurted out that she would send a messenger to her clan to tell them of his abuse.

Seoras had scoffed at her threat, but he must have taken it to heart for he hardly came to her bedchamber afterward and instead spent his lust on comely maidservants. A humiliation in that everyone knew of it, courtiers and his warriors and servants alike—but a welcome one to Cora.

Just thinking of it all again had made her transport herself to a place she never wanted to revisit—not with any man, no, she would not stand for it! She began to struggle, and unfolded her legs to dig at her captor with her heels, but he only drew her closer, aye, so close that she could feel his rampant heartbeat against her back.

That made her fall still even before he hissed in her ear again, Cora fearing that her thrashing might have excited him in some way.

Hot tears squeezed from her eyes—God help her, no man had treated her with love and respect and kindness but Gavin MacLachlan, and he was dead and lost to her forever.

She began to pray harder than she had ever prayed for deliverance, aye, for heaven to open up and smite her so that she wouldn't be made to suffer whatever her captor had in mind for her...

GAVIN FELT the warmth of tears wetting his hand and wanted nothing more than to release Cora—God help him, *Cora!*

He could not believe that he held her in his arms, the last half hour the most intense anxiety he had ever known.

It had been her that he had pulled out of the way of an oxcart's wheels, with the mist and darkness all around them—but he'd had no idea and released the lass he had saved from being crushed, and strode away from her.

Away from her! His driving thought to reach her home to search the place for her—at the point of a sword if anyone defied him.

Yet to his surprise, Cora's father had been the one to open the door at his pounding, the older man's face gone stark white at whomever he had thought it might be—until he recognized Gavin and grabbed his arm to pull him into the main room.

A main room lit only by the flickering flames in the hearth, where Cora's mother stood with her hands clutched to her heart and looked from her husband to Gavin.

"You've come for my daughter?"

The woman's kindly face held such hope, such joy even, that Gavin felt momentarily stunned by their surprising welcome when he had expected to cross swords with Cora's father.

"Aye, but I've little time. Where is she? The mist will lift soon and we must away in the first wagon we find heading back through the gates—"

"She's gone tae the market, MacLachlan!" broke in Owen while Glenis came rushing toward him, her lovely blue eyes—so like Cora's—filled with alarm.

"Aye, did you not see her? She left only moments ago—ah, God, mayhap someone recognized her! We bade her tae hasten tae the market and hide herself in a wagon. We heard last night that the clan council has chosen a husband for her, but Owen and I willna see her suffer again. She's done her part for the Campbells many times over and God only knows when she'll mend from it. Go now, Gavin, you must find her. Take care of our beloved daughter, will you swear it?"

"On my life," Gavin had uttered fiercely, and there had been no time to say more.

Within a moment's time, he had clasped Owen's arm, the two men locking eyes with each other in solemn promise, and then Gavin had headed back out into the damp mist that was fast receding.

His heart thundering in his chest as he had run back toward the market, though a burly guard had demanded his name and tried to stop him by standing in his way.

Gavin's sheathed sword was still wet with the man's blood, his arm tightening around Cora even as her shoulders began to quake with sobs.

Silent sobs, for his hand was still pressed over her mouth, her body tense with fear that made his heart ache to have elicited it in her.

Yet they still weren't far enough away from the stronghold to safely abandon the wagon, aye, another quarter league was needed so that no Campbell guards atop the palisade might see them disembark.

A glance toward his muddy boots where the canvas was lifted a wee bit off the floor of the wagon told Gavin that the day had grown brighter, birds high up in the trees chirping all around them.

A sweet sound as if to mock the gravity of his and Cora's flight from the stronghold. Soon the body of that guard would be discovered in the full light of day and an alarm raised that would send armed warriors thundering on horseback through the gates.

It was a miracle that the farmer's wagon had rumbled past Gavin before he made his way deeper into the market, the canvas covering not flat but with a small lump huddled to one side that told him the angels above had wanted him to find Cora.

The love of his life! The only woman he had ever wanted to wed—aye, tears wetting his own eyes as he had lunged after the wagon and climbed stealthily aboard to bury himself beneath the canvas.

The farmer distracted by counting the coins in his hand and muttering to himself even as he steered his plodding old gelding toward the gates.

Gavin had never known such elation as he drew Cora against him, wanting desperately to murmur her name but certain that she might react so strongly as to draw unwelcome attention toward them.

He had hated covering her mouth with his hand and had felt her jerk in reaction and grow rigid as if she had suffered such an indignity before. That had made him think of Seoras—the man who had stolen from Gavin what he had longed for... their wedding night, when he would have held Cora in his arms and tenderly embraced her, kissed her, and felt the wonder of her innocent body pressed against his—

"Och, God, lass, will you unman me?" Gavin exclaimed in a pained whisper against her ear. Cora had shifted herself and dug her hip bone into his groin so abruptly that he felt a burst of masculine agony.

He had been so lost in lamenting what had been denied him that he had loosened his hold upon her, much to his chagrin. She struggled now as fiercely as a brown sea trout caught in a fisherman's net, which made Gavin decide then and there that their wagon ride must come to an end.

He could smell the salty closeness of the sea that fired his senses as much as holding Cora. They had only to make their way through the forest to the cove where his ship was beached and waiting for them.

A ship as sleek and powerful in cutting through the waves as the legendary Viking ships of old, and as easily pushed back from the rocky shoreline as if they had never taken shelter there. With a grunt of exertion, Gavin grabbed a wriggling Cora and pulled her with him from beneath the canvas, hauling her soundlessly from the wagon, which creaked onward without them and with the farmer none the wiser for the fugitives he'd carried.

She could have screamed, the hood of her cloak fallen away, along with the cap she wore, which loosed her raven hair like a wild tumble around her face.

A face that blanched white as she stared into his eyes, no sound uttering from her pale lips even as she mouthed his name, "Gavin..."

"Aye, lass, forgive me, but it's faster this way," was all he uttered, wanting so desperately to pull her into his arms, but there was no time.

He swept her up and threw her over his right shoulder before she could blink, holding her sweetly rounded rump fast as he lunged with her into the trees.

~

"He's alive... Gavin's alive..." Cora whispered to herself in utter shock, though she clung to him for dear life and tried to keep her head from bouncing against his back.

He careened around tree after tree as if her weight was no burden to him at all, her only view the mossy ground beneath them for the hood falling over her face.

She had no fear of falling, for he held her securely, his hand splayed upon her bottom, which made her face burn and brought back ugly memories of another man's hand callously squeezing her. Pinching her. Spanking her, Seoras's fascination with the practice a demeaning one for it had been painful and cruel. Bile scorched her throat again, but somehow she swallowed it back and tried to think only of Gavin.

Gavin! By some miracle, he had found her... his black woolen cloak rubbing against her flushed cheek making her realize that the man who had grabbed her arm to pull her away from that oxcart's wheels had been no stranger.

No stranger who had strode away from her into the mist while she had hastened toward the market— God in heaven.

He must have gone to her parents' home to find her, cold fear making her grow rigid that he might have challenged her father to fight him. She could feel the hilt of Gavin's sword sheathed beneath his cloak, for it pressed against her arm and made her remember that his prowess with the weapon had earned him a place as a guard in the chieftain's hall.

Her father would be no match for such skill... and her parents had been so adamant about her escaping the stronghold, risking their standing with Clan Campbell and mayhap their lives. No, no, no, they must have told Gavin that she had gone to the market to find a wagon where she could hide, and somehow he had come upon her! Was it when she had dared to stretch out her cramped legs for a moment that he might have spied her shoes peeking from beneath the canvas?

An incredulous laugh burst from her throat that made Gavin slow his pace for an instant, but it held no humor as her shock became a sickening realization that Rory Campbell might discover the truth from her parents. Why had she not considered the depth of their danger until now?

Ah, God, everything was happening so fast, her thoughts in a terrible tumble. The midnight-haired chieftain who held tight reins over much of their clan had sworn that Gavin would be hunted down and killed if he ever came near Cora again—and he wasn't just near but plunging through the trees with her!

"Brody, make ready tae shove away!"

Gavin's roared command made Cora gasp, but she still couldn't see anything more than the ground, though now his boots crunched upon a pebbly beach. The next thing she knew, she was lifted from Gavin's shoulder and hoisted up into the waiting arms of a grim-faced sailor dressed all in black.

"Careful with her, man."

It seemed before Cora had blinked, she found herself standing aboard a black-painted ship that looked massive to her, from its carved prow to its towering mast and wide deck filled with men clambering to obey Gavin's brusque commands.

He had swung himself aboard and stood holding her now, his powerful arm around her waist, and a good thing as the deck seemed to shift beneath her feet.

With great grunts, the crew heaved against black-stained oars that pushed the ship away from the shoreline and into deeper water, everything again happening so swiftly that Cora could but hold onto Gavin's arm in amazement.

Her heartbeat thundering in her ears.

Another realization striking her that there would be no way for Rory and his men to reach them out upon the sea.

Not readily, anyway. The Campbells had ships of

their own, like other Highland clans, and more were being built to aid in King Robert's quest to free Scotland from England's tyranny, but she had never seen any as forbidding as what was clearly Gavin's ship.

She stared awestruck as a great sail was unfurled and billowed out with the wind—a blood-red sail that made her shiver to look upon it.

Only then did she glance up at Gavin to see him looking down at her, his arm tightening possessively around her.

His dark red hair not tied back in a queue but blowing wild and free around his face.

A face so handsome and his eyes so intense a deep brown that her breath caught and her knees seemed to weaken.

Gavin was alive!

The world suddenly spun around her and she collapsed against him... Cora's last conscious thought the sound of Gavin's voice hoarsely calling out her name.

4

"Dinna think you'll rouse her by shaking her," Brody said to Gavin, the helmsman covering Cora to her chin with a blanket. "She's out cold, canna you see? No wonder, the poor lass. You said her parents bade her tae escape the stronghold because another marriage was arranged for her, aye?"

"Aye," Gavin murmured, sitting down upon an iron-banded chest that he had shoved next to the cot where he had laid Cora. His gaze never strayed from her face, which looked ashen in the sputtering glow of an oil lantern. "So her father told me."

"A shock tae the lass, tae be sure. Then she manages tae sneak aboard a wagon only tae have you climb in beside her. Didna you think she mayhap feared for her life, not knowing who you were?"

Gavin shook his head without looking up at the helmsman, though he had spent the last few moments, after carrying Cora into the canvas-covered cargo well, in telling Brody everything that had happened. The man was as gifted in healing as steering the ship, and right now Cora didn't look well at all and might need his help. "I had other things on my mind. .

, like leaving the stronghold in one piece. She might have cried aloud tae know it was me—"

"Even so, another shock for her. Seeing you again after... what was it? A year now?"

"Aye."

"Then she was carried through the woods like a sack of oat flour, all jostled and out of breath. Och, I wouldna be surprised if she sleeps for an hour or more just tae give her poor mind and body a rest. It's best we leave her for now—"

"No, I will stay by her side until she wakes."

Gavin spoke so resolutely that Brody didn't argue with him, though the helmsman clucked his tongue as if displeased.

"You have men awaiting your orders, Laird. Where are we bound? We're already three leagues from shore, so we're safe enough from those Campbells following us—but do we sail north? South?"

Gavin didn't answer, his throat grown tight at Cora's slow, shallow breaths.

She was so beautiful... even more than he remembered. Yet she looked thin, too, the curve of her cheekbones in sharp relief and her skin so pale against the lustrous black of her hair.

Aye, that much hadn't changed... and he fingered a soft curl that made a rush of emotion overwhelm him.

Amazement and mounting concern and intense love for her melding together and nearly choking him as a wetness blurred his eyes, though Gavin lowered his head to hide it from Brody.

Yet the helmsman must have noticed for he cleared his throat, which only made Gavin's feel all the tighter.

"Leave us," he managed to say, though Brody held his ground and muttered a curse.

"Where are we bound, Laird? A port town? The island? You canna think tae keep this beauteous lass for long aboard a ship filled with men—och, now, it wasna said tae arouse your temper!"

Gavin had lunged to his feet to glare at the man, the top of his head scraping the canvas, his hands clenched into fists. "What are you saying, Brody? She'll be in some danger among them? Who have you seen looking at her sideways? Tell me!"

Brody stared at him unperturbed, a low cackle escaping him that only made Gavin bristle further.

For a lean man half his size, the helmsman had never shied away from speaking the truth, his squinty hazel-colored eyes fixed upon Gavin's face.

"I'd follow you anywhere, Laird, but you must take care. The crew is loyal tae you tae a man, but you ask too much of them tae go too long with a comely lass aboard ship. Many of them have wives they havna seen for months. . . while the others, the younger bucks—och, a night's tumble with a wench as soon as we reach a port forever on their minds. Did you consider at all where we might go once you found your lady?"

Gavin stared back, his fists slowly unclenching even as he shook his head.

"So I thought," murmured Brody, shaking his head, too, as he settled upon a three-legged stool on the opposite side of the cot where Cora still slept so soundlessly. "All you've had on your mind since you heard the lass's husband was slain was finding her—and now that she's here, your life is surely tae change. . . and so will ours."

Gavin sank back down onto the iron-banded chest

that held enough gold for fifty men to live upon comfortably for the rest of their lives.

Or at least the thirty men who had thrown in their lots with Gavin—courageous raiders every one of them.

Brody was right. Gavin hadn't thought any further than finding Cora and having her safely by his side, but look at her now.

She had fainted dead away at all the shock and excitement, and they had yet to encounter a ship that might look promising for plunder, which would only stir up more commotion.

Gavin had taken great care not to attack any of King Robert's ships, all of them flying his flag. Yet Gavin had raided other Scots ships aplenty, which had made him a man with a price upon his head among those loyal to England who had suffered losses at his hands.

A man whose capture was eagerly sought by the English as well, though he doubted now that he would ever venture again into their waters. What was the use of it? He possessed everything he needed—by God, he was sitting upon a fortune and with the woman he loved right beside him!

He didn't doubt that Cora's clan might come after him, too, for he knew Rory Campbell was a man who didn't like his plans thwarted.

Gavin could recall several instances, while serving as a guard, when clansmen had disobeyed Rory's commands and found themselves flogged and thrown into a cell at the stronghold prison, and denied food or water for days.

It must have grated so fiercely upon the chieftain—the man at least ten years older than Gavin—and upon those who came before Rory as leaders of the clan, to bow their heads to MacDougall rule in Argyll.

To Earl Seoras's rule. Clearly Rory had been able to stomach it only by arranging a marital alliance that would grant Clan Campbell more power and standing in the Highlands—och, the man might as well have thrown Cora to the wolves!

Gavin could see with his own eyes that she wasn't the same as when he had first held her in his arms in the chapel.

Her lips now bearing only the faintest tinge of color.

Her skin stretched so tightly over her bones.

Her hands with too slender fingers that lay limp at her sides, when before, they had clasped his own with health and vigor as a joyous light shone in her eyes.

Those bluest of blue eyes that had captured his heart from the very first moment his gaze had locked with hers.

Even from the brief moments he'd looked into them again since pulling her out of the wagon, Gavin had seen a dullness there that had made his heart clutch in his chest.

What had Seoras done to her? Gavin remembered like a flash what Brody had said to him earlier that morning.

People change with time—and who can say what the lass suffered while wed tae Earl Seoras?

God help him, Gavin wished he had been the one to sever the bastard's head from his body with a deadly swipe of his sword. One day he would find his way to MacLachlan Castle where his cousin Gabriel now ruled as the earl of Argyll, and thank him personally for delivering Scotland from such a ruthless blight.

And for delivering Cora...

Gavin sighed with heaviness that still she didn't appear any closer to rousing, and he leaned forward to tuck the blanket more snugly around her chin.

Brody was right. His thirty-two-oared birlinn wasn't a fit place for her, not only because of the temptation she might prove to his men but that upon the sea, they were always one ship sighting away from a fight.

It wasn't just the Scotsmen loyal to the new King Edward and the English he'd plundered who wanted to nail his hide to a mast, but other raiders, too, who had lost revenue due to his prowess upon the waves.

One raider in particular wanted him dead—och, such rivalry was to be expected. Gavin had always shrugged it off and laughed into the wind when he and his men left another burning vessel behind them.

Yet now with Cora aboard, the thought that even one precious hair upon her head might be in danger was more than he could stand. Aye, they would head to the island where he and Cora would take temporary refuge while Brody and the crew went back to the mainland for several weeks.

Most of them had come from Ayrshire south of Argyll, and Gavin had kept them too long from their wives and families. Short spells ashore had been enough for those men without such close attachments, but the time had come for him to dole out more gold and allow his crew to decide for themselves if they wanted to continue as raiders or seek a different life.

Just as he needed time to think about what would be best for Cora, aye, where they would go and where they might live.

The island had fresh water and an abandoned

castle half in ruins that rose above the cliffs, while a tiny enclave of monks lived on the leeward side with their shaggy herd of goats. They had afforded Gavin no trouble and kept to themselves, and could provide fresh milk and cheese to him and Cora as they sorted out their plans.

Until a week ago, he had not envisioned anything different for himself than endless raiding well into the future, but now, everything had changed—

"Brody?" Gavin's heart had jumped at Cora's plaintive sigh, but the helmsman only clucked his tongue again as he rose from his stool and laid his weathered hand upon her forehead.

"She's fine, Laird, mayhap only dreaming. So you've decided on the island, then?"

Gavin glanced up sharply at him, but he shouldn't have been surprised Brody had surmised his thoughts. What better course was there if Cora was to leave the ship as soon as possible?

"Aye, steer us tae the southwest. I will stay here with her until she wakes, just as I told you. My thanks, Brody."

The helmsman nodded and without another word, left Gavin alone with Cora as rain began to pelt the canvas.

A good thing the cargo well near the stern was half empty after their stop near Dumfries to unload plunder, except for foodstuffs and casks of fresh water. Just enough room for him and Cora while his men could seek shelter underneath another canvas draped at the center of the ship if a storm erupted, and not come close to her.

He knew masculine lust well and had not denied himself female company when ashore, but now he felt as if he had betrayed her by sleeping with other women when he believed he would never see her again.

"Mayhap you'll forgive me one day," he murmured, wanting so badly to stroke Cora's pale cheek but holding himself back for when she opened her eyes again.

Inwardly, he cursed again that Earl Seoras had been the one to steal her innocence when for Gavin, just holding Cora in his arms in the chapel had been enough to make him tremble.

Her breasts pressed so temptingly against his chest when he had captured her mouth in a kiss, that he'd felt her nipples harden beneath her gown, Cora's breathing grown broken and shallow.

She had desired him as much as he desired her... the promise of their wedding night keeping him awake and restless in the barracks when he should have been sleeping.

All that had been denied him... a niggling of doubt rising up in Gavin that he could not tamp down as Cora sighed again and seemed to stir.

He had gold aplenty and the sultan's jewels, aye, but what sort of life would he truly be able to give her?

Castles were inherited or gifted at the pleasure of the king, whether Scots or English, and he possessed no highborn lineage or favor of any monarch. The crumbling castle on the island would suffice until he decided where he and Cora might set out together, but remaining anywhere so remote would make it impossible for him to hire men to fight for him when needed.

Mayhap the island wasn't such a sound idea after all, considering some of his crew might not wish to leave their families once reunited. Brody would be able to sail the ship back with a skeleton crew—och, what did it all matter now that Cora was at his side? He would find a way forward for them; he *must* find a way, or he would die trying!

Gavin's heart pounding, he could no longer resist and leaned down to press the lightest kiss upon her lips. . . their warmth filling him with exhilaration to have found her.

To have her with him aboard his ship! Days ago he could not have dreamed such a wondrous thing was possible and he kissed her again, only to hear a sharp intake of breath and then the most piercing scream in his ear.

"Get away from me! *God help me, get away from me!*"

5

Cora struggled and kicked beneath what felt like a smothering weight and opened her eyes wide to find Gavin staring down at her.

A look of utter surprise on his face melded with dismay, while she felt as if she were about to be sick.

No one had kissed her since Seoras—ah, God, the memory of his mouth crushing down upon hers, his breath stinking of a rotted tooth and the copious wine he had consumed, was enough to make her retch. She did, too, barely leaning over in time before she vomited upon the floor what little was in her stomach since she hadn't eaten much the night before.

Her head swimming, she held onto the edge of the cot with white-knuckled hands and waited for the terrible sensation to pass, but it didn't and she bent over and retched again.

She could not say if it was the floor pitching beneath her or the hated memories that still pressed in upon her, clouding her brain, but she felt wretchedly ill.

A sour taste in her mouth and her stomach flip-flopping as a crack of thunder seemed to shake the ship—aye, she remembered now!

She had been standing on the deck of a vessel painted all in black with her heart racing and her legs buckling. . . and then everything had faded around her, along with Gavin's voice calling her name.

Gavin...

Somehow she managed to glance over her shoulder to see that he stood now and roared for someone named Brody—aye, she'd heard him shout out that name before, when they had come upon a pebbly beach.

More memories rushed back to her as she squeezed her eyes shut at the throbbing in her head and the floor rocking beneath her, Cora falling back onto the cot and emitting a hoarse groan.

"Do something for her, man!"

Gavin's command a strident one, she heard another voice saying, "The storm, Laird—I need tae be at the helm—"

"I'll steer the ship, Brody, just see tae her."

Another booming crash of thunder and Gavin was gone, Cora half opening her eyes to see that a wiry fellow scurried to one side of the cargo well to grab up an oblong box and then return to the cot. He opened the lid with weather-worn hands and fumbled with small vials until he chose one filled with a dark amber fluid.

"Here, my lady, drink this down."

He didn't wait for her to answer, but fairly shoved the opened vial between her lips and emptied the contents into her mouth—Cora certain she had never tasted so foul a brew. Yet as quickly as the tempest in her stomach had erupted, she felt some relief and stared at Brody in silent thanks.

"Aye, it's ill-tasting stuff, but the seasickness will pass soon, I promise you."

Cora nodded weakly, the cot still pitching beneath her as thunder rumbled and rain drummed upon the canvas. A coarse canvas that Gavin's head had pressed against moments ago, he stood so tall, the expression on his face one of sheer consternation.

A handsome face, so dear, so beloved—no, she would not allow herself to entertain such thoughts ever again... not if she wanted Gavin to live.

Cora lay still while Brody cleaned up the mess on the floor, tucked the blanket more snugly around her, and poured some water into a cup. Then he helped her to lift her head and brought the cup to her parched lips so she could take a sip.

"A wee bit at a time, Lady Cora, or you'll find yourself retching again. Lie back down now and try tae rest."

"I canna see how," she said weakly, clutching the sides of the cot as the ship seemed to plummet deep into a trough and then rise up again. "God help us, surely we're going tae sink!"

"Ah, now, not with your Gavin MacLachlan at the helm, though I'd best go and join him. We'll arrive at the island soon and get you off this ship. It's no fit place for a lass, and thank God he's listened tae me—"

"Island?" Her blurted query sounded like a squawk to Cora, Brody nodding at her.

"Aye, it's well enough out of the way so we'll be safe there and with a protected harbor tae shield us from the worst of the storm—*Lady Cora!*"

She had thrown aside the blanket and bounded from the cot before Brody could catch her, though she heard him lunging after her as she burst out from under the canvas.

Cold rain lashed at her face and near blinded her, but her only thought was to reach Gavin.

She scarcely noticed his men falling back in surprise as she ran past them toward the stern, but she heard Gavin's roar as Brody caught up with her.

"By God, man, *hold her!*"

The helmsman did restrain her with muscled forearms of surprising strength, though Cora struggled to wrench herself away from him.

Her feet slipping and sliding upon the deck as ice-cold waves crashed over the side of the ship, a great boom of thunder making her shriek.

Yet it was the ominous look upon Gavin's face that silenced her. Cora looked up at him through her sodden hair and wet eyelashes as he took her from Brody and swept her into his arms.

His strides as purposeful and solid upon the wet, pitching deck as hers had been unsteady.

She buried her face against his chest as a bright burst of lightning crackled across the gray sky, his heartbeat thudding hard against her ear.

A moment more and he had ducked under the canvas to set her down and rip off the blanket from the cot to wrap her in it.

"Hell and damnation, woman, *what were you thinking?*"

She gulped, never having heard such a harsh tone from him or seen such a black scowl upon his face. She might have thought it wasn't Gavin at all were it not for his physical appearance, as he surely wasn't acting like the man of her memories.

He didn't seem to expect an answer from her, but patted her down from her shoulders to her sodden leather slippers, and then he stood up and yanked away the damp blanket.

"Strip out of your gown, *now!*"

Shivering, she could but stare at him while he

grabbed what she recognized as her fur-lined cloak from where it had been draped over a cask, and shook it out in front of her.

"Strip, Cora, before you catch your death from that wet clothing. You need something dry and warm around you. Do as I say, lass, or I'll rip the gown from you myself—"

"A-aye, then, I'll oblige you." Her hands trembling with cold and her teeth chattering, Cora felt again as if she were looking at a stranger to see Gavin's gaze still so furious.

His eyes darkened and as turbulent as the foul weather howling outside the canvas while she hastened to obey him... though a blush raced from her scalp to her toes a moment later when she stood naked and covered in goosebumps in front of him.

Yet not for long as Gavin whisked the cloak around her and tightened it like a cocoon, and then bodily lifted her and settled her upon the cot.

His hands in a vise-like grip upon her upper arms as he shook her, not once but twice and so roughly that Cora was certain her teeth rattled.

"Never do that again aboard a ship—*any ship!*—if a storm is raging," he grated out in a stark voice she didn't recognize. "You could have been swept overboard by the waves. You could have slipped on the deck and struck your head. Thank God, Brody caught up with you, but I've never seen the poor man's face so stricken. He was as white as a sheet and the rest of my men staring like startled sheep and forgetting their duties—at the height of a thunderstorm!"

Cora gulped at such vehemence, such wrath, the Gavin she had known disappeared altogether beneath a forbidding countenance that was truly alarming to behold.

Tears jumped to her eyes and she fumbled to say something, which only elicited a blistering curse from him. He finally let go of her arms and straightened to his full height to stare down at her.

Still angry, but a flash of regret crossing his face, too, as he seemed to force himself to take a deep breath. Then another breath, some of the tension visibly easing from his broad shoulders as he shook his head and tunneled his fingers through his wet hair.

"Cora. . ." came his measured voice that held a trace of apology, though his expression was still grim. "Why did you run out like that—scaring the devil from me? If you'd fallen into the sea with those waves, I would never have been able tae save you. . ."

His voice caught and he fell silent, while Cora felt remorse flood her.

She *had* done a rash and thoughtless thing, and she felt terrible for causing him such distress, which only heightened her awareness of the depth of his feelings for her. Yet she could not fall sway to them!

The deadly threat to Gavin from her kinsmen still remained, though thankfully he hadn't drowned as she had been led to believe, but stood alive and whole in front of her. To think of the grief she had suffered and tears she had shed—ah, God, she could not bear such sorrow again.

She was poison to Gavin if she didn't part from him, and she wanted him to live. Cora lifted her chin to stare back at him though she felt, once again as in the chapel a year ago, her heart was breaking in two. . .

"Brody said we're bound for an island—but I dinna want tae go there, Gavin. I'm grateful tae you for helping me, but I-I dinna want tae be with you. . ."

Cora faltered at the sudden look of pain that

crossed his face, though somehow she managed to find her voice again and rush on.

"It's a convent where I must go. I'm not the same as you remembered me and never will be. My father told me he would send a messenger tae King Robert at Dumbarton Castle and ask him tae intervene with my clan and spare me from another marriage. I only want peace and a quiet life—mayhap that of a nun, can you understand? We once swore our love for each other, but it wasna meant tae be. I'm freeing you, Gavin, tae find another and know some happiness—"

"Freeing me?"

Cora nodded, feeling a burst of unease at the harshness in his voice and the hard set of his jaw.

Yet it was Gavin's eyes burning into hers with renewed anger that made her glad for the cot beneath her, aye, she was certain her knees would have given way.

Something else was reflected there, too, something akin to anguish though it was gone as soon as he stepped closer to her.

"You're mistaken as tae my intent here, Cora Mac-Dougall—"

"Dinna call me by that name. I hate it! *Hate it!*" Cora glared at him now, too, stung that he would have so purposely spat out what she never wished to be called again. Surely he knew that as a widow, she had gone back to her clan name even as she had returned to her parents' home. "I'm Cora Campbell, just as you knew me before—"

"Aye, when you chose tae marry another man instead of me. A wealthy man. A powerful man. Were you toying with me all those months, lass? A wee dalliance tae while away the hours? You fled from me that last time so quickly, as if you feared me seeing the truth of it in your eyes."

Cora stared at him in shock, the man she'd known with his tender kisses, warm embraces, and whispers of love missing from this forbidding Highlander standing so close to her. Surely he didn't believe that of her? Yet what did it matter now if it would make him hate her? Aye, that would be far better than a cursed love that would condemn him to an early grave.

"So you've no answer for me."

His voice sounded flat now, almost empty of emotion, though his large hands were clenched at his sides.

"I-I never wanted tae marry you. . . of course you must have known!" Cora blurted, wanting to have it out and done, her heart aching at the falsehood she conjured. "A dalliance, aye. I was always intended for a highborn lord. You were nothing but a fisherman when we met, Gavin. . . and only later became one of the chieftain's guards. A MacLachlan, to be sure, but with no more tae your name than the sword you carried—"

"*Enough!*"

Gavin's roar as loud and fierce to Cora's ears as the thunderclap overhead, she knew she had wounded him deeply and she lowered her head, tears filling her eyes.

Tears she didn't want him to see. . . scalding tears for him and for her and the love they had once shared, burned down to ashes.

All he had to do now was sail to Dumbarton where he would let her off the ship and she could make her way to the convent until it was time to face King Robert.

Mayhap by now the messenger was already on his way southward, which would be a good thing, considering Rory and her clansmen might already be looking for her.

They would have gone to her parents' door with news of her impending marriage to that northern laird and found her missing. Her father and mother hopefully, for their sakes, pleading no knowledge of her departure. She had disappeared as if a phantom, with nothing to point to Gavin in any way helping her to escape...

"You might care tae know that your clansmen will have found the body by now and an alarm will have been raised."

"*Body?*" Cora looked up to meet the coldness in Gavin's eyes, her lips forming into a hoarse whisper. "Dear God, my father?"

Relief plummeted through her when Gavin shook his head, his voice as cold as his gaze.

"A guard who stood in my way until I cut him down, but it matters naught tae me if your clansmen suspect I'm at the heart of it. I found you and have you now, the time for retribution begun. There will be no marital alliance for the Campbells tae strengthen their power in Argyll. Nor will you wear the habit of a nun... since you will become my bride."

"Bride?" Cora echoed, feeling certain then and there that Gavin was no longer the man she remembered, either. As his gaze swept her from head to foot, his expression chillingly ruthless, she began to shiver uncontrollably and it wasn't because she was still damp and naked beneath the cloak. "Surely y-you canna mean tae force me tae marry you—"

"I'll do whatever I must tae thwart your clan and gain my revenge. They'll curse the day they cast me from the stronghold as if I was nothing tae them. Kicked and pummeled, my sword taken from me, the breacan stripped from my back. When Rory's men came looking for me the next morning tae see if I'd heeded them and fled, I barely managed tae steal a fishing boat and head out tae sea—but they didna defeat me. It wasna love that spurred me tae find you when I heard you'd been made a widow, but hatred, and dinna ever forget it!"

The canvas was flung back and Gavin disappeared outside into the raging storm before Cora could utter a word, his words stunning her to the quick.

How could she have been so wrong about him? What depth of feeling had she imagined?

Here she had meant to spare Gavin a terrible fate at the hands of her clan by spurning him, but it had only made him reveal what lay at the heart of him appearing back in her life.

Vengeance. Hate.

Not love. . . not love, dear God in heaven, protect her.

6

"Steer tae the southeast, Brody!"

Gavin wiped away the rain from his eyes and peered into the darkness of the storm, an ugly realization near choking him.

Cora didn't love him.

She had never loved him. It had only been words... *empty words*!

It was true, then. She *had* agreed to wed another man for clan and honor. No coercion. No treachery. Yet she must have indeed suffered during that marriage; her father had told Gavin as much that morning and he had seen himself the changes wrought in her since they were last together. The specter of another husband chosen for her by her clan had spurred her to flee—her own parents aiding her—and now she was speaking of becoming a nun.

A nun! His beautiful Cora, except she wasn't his... unless Gavin forced her to marry him.

Could he do it? Would he do it? The thought sickened him. His fists tightened with fury at himself for his harshness toward her, but she could have been swept overboard in the blink of an eye and swallowed by the boiling sea.

Even now the storm lashed at the ship, the wind whipping sheets of rain across the deck that felt like icy needles against his face.

How else could he have impressed upon her the folly of her action than to speak so severely to her? He must have frightened her—but by God, he had wanted to scare some sense into her.

He had seen the tears brimming in her eyes. Had his infuriated display reminded her of her slain husband?

That thought sickened Gavin even further and he pounded his fist upon the wet railing as Brody shouted beside him.

"Did you say tae the southeast, Laird? The island lies directly tae the west only a half league away—"

"Southeast, man, *southeast!*"

A strange look clouded Brody's face, but then he heaved against the helm to turn the ship straight into the wind.

The sail billowed out like a blood-red cloud while some of the men pulled hard at ropes and others clambered out from beneath the flapping canvas of their makeshift shelter.

Thankfully the strength of the storm appeared to be lessening within the last few moments, but it was nothing to the tempest raging inside Gavin.

I dinna want tae be with you...

Something had snapped inside him to hear Cora say those words, the pain so intense that he had lashed out in fury.

A desperate plan erupting in his brain.

A wild accusation flying from his lips—and he had gotten his answer.

I never wanted tae marry you... of course you must have known!

So she had admitted to him after he had accused her of toying with him. She had looked stunned at his query, as if reluctant to reveal the truth, but then he had pressed her and she had burst out with words that made him clench his jaw in anguish.

Why had he not guessed that he was a mere dalliance to her? A lovesick fool holding onto a dream of one day taking Cora for his wife. . . when she had never looked upon him as anything other than a man far beneath her. Aye, the only way he would have her would be to force her to become his bride—God help him, the woman he loved!

Gavin spun around to stare at the cargo well where he'd left Cora, that canvas tamped down more securely and holding up against the storm.

A dim golden glow shone through the thick fabric, the oil lantern still lit, and he imagined Cora must be huddled on the cot, trying to stay warm.

"I hope you gave the lass dry clothes after you ordered her tae strip, Laird."

Gavin glanced sharply at Brody, whose expression appeared grim and disapproving, his face streaked with rain.

"You heard me even with the storm?"

"Aye, when your voice was raised and that was often enough. It's only canvas after all and no thick wall."

Now Gavin sensed a clear rebuke in Brody's voice, which made him bristle. "She's wrapped up tight in her cloak—"

"Och, it's not enough. Will you have her catch her death just because you're furious with her? You know there's extra clothing in that chest by the cot. Men's tunics, aye, but after the chill of the rain, another warm garment against her skin would be a wise thing."

Brody fell silent while Gavin scowled at him, though he felt a stab of concern.

"Very well, I'll tend tae her, but then I'll be back straightaway. Hold tae the course I gave you and steer us tae the shore and the nearest village. It's a church and a priest I'm seeking—"

"So you're going through with this madness—och, Laird, you'll lose her forever if you force her into a marriage. She's in a terrible state, canna you see? One shock after another and now you raging at her and threatening tae wed her as vengeance against her clan. I thought you cared for the lass—aye, loved her!"

Gavin stared at Brody in disbelief.

The helmsman forthrightly speaking his mind was one thing, Gavin had always valued him for it, but he had gone too far with this vehement reproach.

Surely he didn't know the full story, for he couldn't have overheard everything, Cora had spoken so softly at times. What of *her* words to Gavin?

"I love her, but she doesna love me," he muttered as a gust of wind buffeted against him. The rain had stopped, the sky brightening to the west, but waves still rocked the ship and Gavin had to brace his feet wide to keep his balance. "Didna you hear her cry out that she never wanted tae marry me?"

"Aye, what of it? If you hadna felt something deep and strong between you, you wouldna have wasted your time in trying tae find her—vengeance or no. Dinna torture yourself over words, Laird. What do her eyes say when she looks at you? That's what you must heed—och, what do I know? The sea's always been my mistress—and there's a half dozen women that have cursed me for it."

Brody had glanced away from him to stare out

across the white-capped waves while Gavin wondered indeed, if the helmsman knew of what he spoke.

Cora's outburst still burned in his brain... but what about when she had lowered her head, her eyes filled with tears.

Tears that had trickled down her pale cheeks, though she had quickly wiped them away as if not wanting him to see them.

Not wanting him to see them...

"Did the lass tell you where she wished tae go?"

Gavin met Brody's gaze at the heartening realization that what Cora had said to him and what she felt might be two different things entirely. Anything was possible, aye?

"She longs for the peace of a convent."

"A convent? I'm not surprised after what she's borne—"

"Nor I, but that's the last place I'll take her. She said her father was sending a plea tae King Robert tae intervene with her clan and spare her from another marriage. It wouldna be hard tae find him if he's quartered at Dumbarton Castle—at least that's where Cora said the messenger was bound."

"Aye, or mayhap he's already marched tae the south or north, the man has enemies tae rout wherever he goes. We'll know once we sail there... unless it's still a church and a priest that you're eager tae find."

A weighty silence fell between them, the wind no more than a stiff breeze now and the dark clouds faded away to reveal a clear expanse of blue.

It never ceased to amaze Gavin how the weather could change from one moment to the next... much like the change of heart that made him feel an oppressive brute to have threatened Cora with a forced marriage.

He could never do such a thing to her no matter he longed for revenge against her kinsmen.

He wanted her not to be frightened.

He wanted her to be freed forever from the schemes of her clan.

He wanted her lovely face to not be so thin and her skin so pale.

He wanted to see her blue eyes shining bright again and to see her smiling... at him.

He wanted to hear again that she loved him and know without a doubt that she meant every word.

Was such a miracle too much to hope for? How would it ever come to pass unless he did everything he could to ease her heart and mind?

Aye, he would take her to King Robert and not even wait for a messenger. Who could say if her father would be able to send one now? For all Gavin knew, Cora's parents might be locked in a dank cell at this very moment for the part they had played in her escape as Rory Campbell decided what punishment to mete out—

"Bastard," Gavin grated under his breath, which made Brody look at him with some alarm.

"Me, Laird?"

"No. *Me*, tae have been so harsh with her." Gavin met Brody's eyes, feeling humbled by the man. "You're a trusted friend and I'm grateful tae you. She deserves far better than I gave her. Pity, aye, and patience—"

"Kindliness, too, Laird, you willna win her without it. So we're bound now for Dumbarton?"

Gavin nodded, cuffing the helmsman on the shoulder as the crew erupted into the commotion of setting the ship to rights after the storm.

Brooms sweeping water from the deck. Ropes tightened and overturned casks righted. The canvas under which many of them had sought shelter rolled up and stowed alongside the railing.

The waves, so dark and threatening not long ago, glistened in the brilliant sunlight as some of the men began to whistle and hum.

Brody gave a laugh and eased up his grip upon the helm, the sea so much calmer, but then he clucked his tongue and shook his head.

"I dinna want tae harbor the notion, but what if King Robert hasna time for a matter such as Lady Cora's and decides tae send her back tae her clan?"

Eager to return to the cargo well, Gavin had already entertained that possibility and shrugged it off.

"He's known as a fair man and I've done naught tae earn his wrath—och, more his praise for plundering my share of English ships. I've another way tae sway him, too, a chestful of gold tae make him hear Cora's side of things. Once she's free of her kinsmen and the king grants her the right tae choose her own course, mayhap she'll feel differently about spending the rest of her life in a convent."

"Aye, Laird, we'll hope for it," Brody said over his shoulder, Gavin already striding across the deck.

Considering how furious he'd been when he left the cargo well, he felt almost embarrassed to face her and angry at himself all over again.

Yet he stopped just before ducking under the canvas, stricken at the heart-wrenching sound of weeping —God help him, *Cora.*

He lunged into the cargo well in a rush, only to hear a startled scream much like when he had kissed her.

After the bright daylight outside, it took a moment

for him to adjust his eyes to the dimness, even with the oil lantern sputtering atop a barrel.

His heart lurched to see that the cot was empty, the blanket he'd used to pat her dry and her sodden gown clumped in a heap upon the wooden planking.

"Cora?"

He heard soft sobs off to one side, and glimpsed a pair of slippered feet disappearing beneath the hem of her cloak as if she thought she could hide from him—though she sat huddled between two water casks.

Her head bowed so he couldn't see her face, while her sobs became sniffles and then fell silent altogether but for the broken sound of her breathing.

Gavin felt wretched. *He* had done this to her with his bluster and fury and cruel threat to wed her against her will, so why wouldn't she have been weeping?

"Cora, the storm is past. Brody. . . the man who helped you earlier when you felt so sick, reminded me that we've extra clothing you can use. You must be cold even with your cloak. I'll hang your gown out on the deck tae dry in the sun, but until you can wear it again, I want tae give you a tunic tae keep you warm—"

"I dinna want anything from you. Leave me in peace. . . please!"

7

Cora clamped her mouth shut, hoping desperately that Gavin would heed her though she'd heard him venture closer.

Yet she couldn't stifle a hiccough that erupted in her throat, which felt raw from weeping.

Useless weeping that had done nothing for her other than to draw Gavin back into the cargo well—ah, God, what would he do to her now? Haul her to her feet and rip the cloak from her body so she would be forced to don whatever he offered her?

"Cora, here, I'll fetch it for you. It's a man's tunic, but you'll find it dry and warm."

She flinched at the sound of a chest lid thrown back, and then she heard a low curse as he rummaged around and seemed not to find what he was seeking.

"Blankets... where the devil?"

Cora gasped as another chest lid was thrown back with a thud, but no more cursing as she heard his footfalls once again coming closer.

"You canna sit there on the floor, you'll catch a chill. Here, take the tunic."

She flinched again as a garment brushed against

her leg, Cora's heart beating faster that Gavin stood right over her.

"Please, Cora. If not for me, then for Brody. He's worried for you—"

"I dinna want his concern nor yours. Please leave me alone!"

Her voice sounding as scratchy as her throat felt at raising her voice, she buried her face against her knees, which were hugged to her chest.

Mayhap if she squeezed her eyes shut, she could will him away and wake from this terrible dream that her life had become.

She held her breath and counted silently to herself, hoping... hoping...

"Cora, I willna leave until I know you're dressed warmly and back upon the cot. I'll turn away if it will make you feel better—"

"There is naught tae make me feel better than you honoring my request tae take me tae the convent near Dumbarton! If you promise me as much, aye, then, I'll stand up and don your accursed tunic."

Silence fell in the cargo well, no response at all coming from Gavin though she could hear his men walking across the deck and, unbelievably—the sound of singing.

Singing, while she had wept her eyes out in this dim, stuffy space that smelled of salted fish, lamp oil, and tarred wood.

It amazed her still that water hadn't washed inside, considering the ferocity of the storm, but what did she know of ships and their construction? Thankfully the canvas had held taut and firm no matter the comings and goings of Brody and Gavin and herself, when she had lunged outside into lashing wind and rain.

Remorse stabbed her at remembering Gavin's

harsh rebuke that seemed to still ring in her ears, along with his intention to force her into marriage.

Force her!

At once any guilt she felt for whatever consternation she had cost him disappeared altogether, his continued silence making her wonder if he might have quietly departed from the cargo well.

Was that all she had to do to make him leave her in peace? Screech at him indignantly and refuse to oblige him in any way? She thought to lift her head and peek, but a low rumble of chuckling made her freeze with her face still buried against her knees.

Was he laughing at her? Here she felt heartsick at all that had occurred and all that had been said with no sign of things getting better than his unexpected offer of a tunic.

The man she loved had become a monster! So cold and callous and unfeeling that he would mock her while she huddled, shivering, on the floor of the cargo well—

"You willna go tae a convent, Cora Campbell, but I promise tae take you tae King Robert. Will that please you?"

She didn't lift her head, so stunned that she didn't move at all.

She just sat there and wondered if she had misheard him or he was toying with her. Aye, he was playing a cruel game and deriving great satisfaction from her misery and shock that he intended to wed her out of vengeance.

What had happened to the Gavin MacLachlan she had known and once so happily wanted to marry? Yet as soon as she asked herself that question, Cora knew the answer, even as she heard him slowly exhale as if losing patience with her.

She was much to blame for the unhappy changes in him, and she knew it.

She had broken his heart that fateful day in the chapel, even if she had done the only thing she could to save his life.

She had considered telling him the truth and the two of them attempting an escape from the stronghold, but she had been watched so closely that fleeing together would have been impossible. Her clansmen would have cut him to pieces before they reached the gates. Instead she had run away from him and left him standing there alone, even though he had called out her name and it had been all she could do not to return to him—

"Cora, did you hear me?"

She started at the low intensity in his voice; Gavin wasn't chuckling anymore. Slowly she lifted her head to look at him, his face so handsome in the flickering lamplight that her breath caught and an intense yearning filled her.

A yearning for what they had once been to each other—och, had it been only a year ago? She had lived a lifetime since then with her wretched marriage to Seoras and her empty existence as a countess that had so mercifully come to an end two months ago at his death.

She had been so proud of her clansmen coming to the aid of King Robert alongside Gabriel MacLachlan, now the ruling earl in Argyll, while her cousins Cameron and Conall Campbell had been made barons and the lairds of their own castles for helping to save the king's life.

What would they say to Gavin's plans for her? What would they say to her clan's intention to wed her off again? A clan that she felt now had betrayed her while Gavin intended to use her as mercilessly for his own ends. No, she could no more believe that he intended to take her to the king after how ruthlessly he had treated her today than she and Gavin could ever go back to how things had been before.

"You lie."

Cora saw more than a flicker of anger in Gavin's darkened gaze at her low utterance. He stiffened in front of her, his hand tightly gripping the tunic he had offered to her.

"I dinna lie, woman. You wish for King Robert tae intervene with your clan on your behalf, aye?"

She nodded, her heartbeat racing at the gravity in Gavin's voice and how intently he stared at her.

"Upon reconsideration, I believe it would be a wise step for you tae make your plea tae the king and end your clan's hold upon you once and for all. Then we can discuss what's tae come afterward. I'm sure he's very busy with matters of war on his mind, but I guarantee, Cora, you will be heard."

He sounded so resolute, so sure of himself, she stared at him with her mind racing and her heart thundering in her ears—though still, she did not believe him.

"You hold some special place with King Robert tae make such an assurance? I could have sworn I heard Brody call you Laird. Have you risen so far, then? You're one of the king's captains?"

Cora bit her lip at the sudden scowl on Gavin's face, and knew she had opened a fresh wound at how carelessly she had phrased her query.

Only a short while ago she had told him she'd never intended to marry him because he wasn't a highborn lord—aye, a falsehood, but what else could she have said to spurn him? Yet with this vast ship and so large a crew, it was clear Gavin had come far during the last year. How else if not with the favor of the king?

"I owe what I have tae no one but myself," he bit off as if he had read her mind, tossing the tunic at her feet. "Brody calls me Laird out of respect and because it suits him." Within one stride he went to an ironbanded chest near the cot and threw back the lid, the contents making Cora gasp and her eyes grow wide.

She had never seen so much gold, aye, never knew so much even existed.

The coins glittered in the lamplight, but just as abruptly, Gavin slammed the lid shut while Cora could but gaze at him in utter astonishment.

"Who are you?" she murmured, his scowl still fierce, though he returned to stand in front of her. "*What* are you?"

"A raider, and this is *my* ship. *My* crew. Not a plank or nail belongs to King Robert nor a single gold coin, but I'll offer him all of what's in that chest if he'll free you forever from Clan Campbell. Now. . . how does that please you?"

Cora couldn't speak, she was so stunned, though Gavin reached down and pulled her to her feet.

Not roughly, but not gently, either, the grip of his hands on her arms making her wince even as he released her.

"I swore tae your mother *on my life* that I would take care of you, which means an audience with the king. It's what your father wanted for you, aye? Yet if you catch a chill, mayhap you willna survive until morning, which is how long it will take us tae reach Dumbarton. Will you don this blasted tunic, Cora?"

She sucked in her breath, her eyes wide as he swept up the garment and shoved it into her hand.

Then he crossed his arms across his chest and stood there silently, watching, waiting...

"A-aye, I'll wear it." Cora's hands trembled as she slipped the cloak from her shoulders, her eyes never leaving Gavin's face as his gaze remained fixed upon her.

Not her body, now covered in goosebumps from the cool air as she shook out the crumpled tunic and then pulled it over her head.

Only her face, which now burned from his scrutiny, a heavy sigh escaping him when she had once again donned the cloak.

"Do you feel warmer?"

"Aye...much."

He shook his head as if he couldn't believe the battle that had ensued to get her to oblige him, and heaved another sigh.

"There's a bucket in the corner when you need tae relieve yourself. I dinna want you above deck with the crew. Brody will return shortly tae gather a plate of food for you."

"I'm not hungry."

"Then make yourself eat... even if only an oatcake. You're the most beautiful lass I've ever seen, but too thin by far. I dinna want King Robert tae think I've mistreated you in any way. I'm a raider, aye, but no fool. I've not destroyed any of his ships nor put any of his men tae the sword. It will serve me well for him tae keep that good impression of me and my crew. Now get some rest."

Rest? Her head spun with unsettling images of vessels aflame and men screaming, with Gavin at the center of the carnage...and a chest filled with gold that might as well be stained red with blood.

A raider. She had heard of such men and their violent exploits upon the sea during banquets in Seoras's great hall... and there had been one man in particular of that ilk who had even feasted at their head table.

A huge, swarthy man with greasy dark hair that had made her shudder to look upon him, he was so coarse and unwashed and clearly hadn't cared at all that his stench overpowered even the smell of food. She couldn't remember his name other than that he was a MacDougall, and she shuddered to think of him now, which made Gavin reach out to take her arm.

"Here... let me help you."

His stern tone had softened, much as he had sounded when he had reappeared in the cargo well. It wasn't a shudder of repulsion again that coursed through her at his touch, but a shiver from her head to her toes.

Cora felt her face flush anew as he led her back to the cot and helped her to sit down, though he released her at once as if thinking she might protest his attention.

Why wouldn't he after all she had said to him? He must truly think her a grasping woman indeed after her unthinking comment about his rise in the world—aye, and how she'd gaped at all the gold—which made her so sad of a sudden that she slumped upon the cot.

"Cora?"

"I'm weary, Gavin... but my thanks for the tunic. Dinna trouble yourself any further about me—"

"An impossible thing, woman, so dinna ask it of me," he cut her off, though not harshly.

Then he was gone after grabbing up her gown, the canvas falling back in place and Cora once again alone as Gavin's roar seemed to echo aboard the ship.

"We sail for Dumbarton, men! Throw your backs into those ropes and hoist the sail higher."

She could hear the deck erupting in commotion, his crew obeying him instantly. Why wouldn't they with so formidable a commander as Gavin issuing orders?

A raider. She still could not believe it. From everything she had heard about them and seen from that disgusting man who had held favor with Seoras, they were bloodthirsty and cruel and avaricious—and only interested in their own gain.

Yet Gavin planned to offer that chest filled with gold coins to King Robert so her clansmen could never force her into another marriage. Why? Vengeance? Mayhap that would satisfy his lust for retribution to have thwarted them, but who could say?

All Cora knew was that she felt drowsy of a sudden. The tunic against her skin so warm and the ship rocking in so strangely soothing a manner that she lay down on her side upon the cot and arranged her cloak over her.

Her eyes were closed before she settled her head in the crook of her arm, although one last thought taunted her.

What had Gavin meant about discussing what came afterward once she was free of her clan? He may have reconsidered taking her to Dumbarton, if not the convent, but did he still intend to force her into marrying him?

That possibility brought on another shiver, and Cora drew the cloak more tightly around her shoulder.

Such a wedding would free her from her clan, too. . . so he didn't really need to take her to the king. Why was he doing it, then? Was it simply his vow to her mother that fueled him? If so, that would make him less of a monster and more like the Gavin she remembered—ah, God, her mind spun from all of it and she so wanted to sleep.

Her freedom from her kinsmen's plans for her, however gained, wouldn't stop them from hunting Gavin down and murdering him just as they vowed a year ago. There could be no marriage, *ever*, forced or otherwise, which brought a terrible ache to Cora's heart, she couldn't deny it.

Unless there was some way she could make a plea to King Robert for Gavin's sake as well.

8

"What did those sniveling monks have tae say? Do they know where Gavin Mac-Lachlan buried his spoils on the island?"

"They claim tae know nothing, Laird. Nothing! One of them pissed himself and fell tae the ground, babbling that he spied a ship eastward with a blood-red sail five days ago, but they didna make land."

Ranulf MacDougall swore vehemently at this news and then broke wind as violently, which made the man in front of him gasp and his eyes water.

A blood-red sail... that arrogant bastard. Insolent whelp! He had been a renowned raider for ten years before Gavin had come along and plundered the best and richest ships, aye, English and Scots ships that should have fallen prey to Ranulf and his crew.

It was *his* gold that he believed Gavin had hidden somewhere on this remote island fit for no more than a dozen aging monks and their pitiful herd of goats.

"Bring him tae me." With that terse command, Ranulf waved away the crewman and strode to the cliff in three strides that would have taken an ordinary-sized man eight or nine, but he was no ordinary man.

He was bigger and taller and heavier than most, his great girth not fat at all but solid muscle. Some called him a giant with fear and trembling in their voices, and even his own mother had cursed him at his birth for tearing her asunder.

A mother that had been a cousin to Seoras Mac-Dougall, which had made Ranulf and the slain earl blood kin. He sorely missed those nights of carousing in the great hall of the MacDougall fortress—och, not under that clan's banner any longer but given over to a Campbell at the behest of King Robert, the devil take them all!

Ranulf hated that false king.

He hated the Campbells for rising up and helping to vanquish their rightful overlord, Earl Seoras. Ranulf would have done anything to support his cousin's ambition to become King of Scots, but Seoras had been murdered while Ranulf was out at sea, raiding and searching for that red-haired upstart known as the devil of the seas.

Aye, most of all he hated Gavin MacLachlan, whose true name he had learned a week ago by an unexpected twist of fortune.

Before then, Ranulf had known him by the name that only *he* deserved after long terrorizing the English coastline as well as ships belonging to Scotsmen loyal to England. He had held no allegiance to King Edward, now rotting in his grave, nor did he support his mewling son, another Edward. Ranulf had wanted Seoras to rule Scotland, and mayhap one day England, too.

"We would have grown as rich as Solomon together," he muttered as he gazed out upon a sea grown calm again after a fierce storm that had nearly dashed his ship upon the rocks.

They had taken refuge in the harbor, but the wind had proved so wild and the waves so rough that their anchor had barely held against the squall. Yet the rain had ceased and the sky returned to blue, allowing his men to once again fan out across the island in search of buried treasure—*his* treasure.

"*Devil of the seas*, my stinking arse." Ranulf broke wind that sounded like a bleating horn, and if he hadn't been so incensed that their hunt thus far had proved fruitless, he might have thrown back his head and laughed.

He was the true devil of the seas, and not that cocky newcomer. Ranulf intended to find the gold and then track down Gavin and throttle the breath from him until his tongue turned purple.

"Then I'll cut him into wee bits and feed his flesh tae the sharks, along with his men!" Ranulf roared at the top of his lungs, a gust of wind lifting his long, unkempt hair.

Little did Gavin know that a drunken, loose-lipped member of his crew had revealed much to a harlot during an overnight stay in Dumfries no more than a week ago. She had shared her newfound knowledge with Ranulf a few nights later after a rousing tumble that made him grow hard at thinking about her huge, bobbing breasts.

Rock-hard and erect and eager for another tumble —och, where was a wench when he had need of one?

He would have brought her aboard his ship if he hadn't decided it was better to cut her throat so she wouldn't spill her secrets to any other patrons of his ilk.

She had sworn when he'd drawn his knife that she had told only him since she knew of his reputation and that he would reward her well with a fat purseful of coins, and Ranulf believed her. Truth seemed to spill out of folk when they knew they were going to die.

He had believed her, too, when she had vowed with desperation in her eyes that she wouldn't tell another soul. Yet he had no desire to risk a horde of raiders descending upon the island to search for what rightfully belonged to him.

No wonder Gavin had chosen this out-of-the-way place to hide his spoils... and it would have remained perfect for that purpose if his sotted crewmember hadn't revealed its location and more while lying sated between that harlot's thighs.

Aye, MacLachlan's true name, and that two chests filled with coins had already been buried there earlier in the year.

Ranulf had learned, too, that he hadn't been able to find him for months because Gavin had spent the summer raiding in the waters near Normandy. The coastlines of England and Scotland hadn't been rich enough for that blasted pup!

Gavin and his crew had only docked outside Dumfries two days before Ranulf—och, he couldn't believe how narrowly he had missed him.

"So close... so close," he grated under his breath, wondering if Gavin had any clue that his crewman had betrayed him.

If Ranulf had a traitor aboard his ship and discovered his disloyalty, he would string him up and cut him from his breastbone to his navel and watch his bloody entrails spill out upon the deck. Then he would slice out his wagging tongue while he still lived, a lingering death the only fit punishment for such a crime.

Ranulf almost pitied Gavin for the treachery that

no raider should suffer from one of his men... *almost*. He snorted with derision and spun around to face his crewman, who hauled a thin-faced monk toward him, the man sobbing and his brown robe wet and stinking of urine.

"You're the one that saw a ship with a blood-red sail?"

"Aye, Laird, far away, they never came close —aagh!"

Ranulf had grabbed him by the throat and carried him toward the cliff, where he held him with his bare feet grazing the ground, only inches away from the precipice.

"Never came close, you say? I dinna believe you."

The monk gulped and gasped for air as Ranulf's huge hand tightened around his neck, but when he swung him out over the edge—a choked shriek rent the air.

"No, no, no, they did make land! Spare me, Laird, *spare me!*"

With a howl of disgust, Ranulf stepped backward and hurled the monk to the ground. "Speak, man!"

"T-they anchored in the harbor. It was already g-growing dark so I headed back tae the other side of the island. I had no lantern and the footpaths are treacherous. If they buried anything, Laird, I didna see it, I swear tae you on this cross!"

With shaking fingers, the monk held out a crucifix carved in wood that hung from a leather cord around his neck, and once again began to sob—which made Ranulf curse violently.

He hated weeping. He hated weakness. He thought to silence the man that very moment by hurling him from the cliff, but what good would that do him?

"Get him out of my sight."

Two crewmen rushed forward to oblige him, while the monk appeared to have wet himself again, he was so terrified.

Good. Ranulf wanted him to be so frightened that he would blather to the others, and one or two might step forward in fear for their lives with something useful to tell him... something they had seen or something they had heard.

Those chests had to be here somewhere—damn the downpour that had beaten down the soil and erased any tracks Gavin and his men might have made. Mayhap the gold hadn't been buried at all, but was hidden in a cave or beneath a cache of rocks covered by waves at high tide—

"Laird, *look*!"

A wide-eyed crewman pointing out to sea, Ranulf spun around to the cliff, his heart lurching in his chest.

By God, it couldn't be... but there it was, a blood-red sail about a half league from the island, though the ship wasn't headed in their direction.

Instead the prow was turned toward the southeast, though Ranulf was certain Gavin couldn't have spied his own ship anchored in the harbor for the dense trees.

No, something told him they must have been headed for the island to have ventured so close, and then had switched course—but why?

"To the ship—*now*!"

His bellowed command echoing around him, Ranulf nearly knocked over several of his men in his haste to lunge down the hill, the ground shaking beneath his heavy footfalls.

"You'll not elude me this time, MacLachlan," he

vowed through gritted teeth, his breathing hard. "I'll drag you back here and *you* will lead me to the treasure, I swear it!"

∽

"She's snug and warm now, Laird?"

Gavin nodded at Brody, who had watched him with great interest as he carefully arranged Cora's gown over the railing to dry.

A dark blue gown that had hung upon her too loosely, even when soaking wet, which made him hope that she would heed his advice and try to eat, no matter she had said she wasn't hungry.

"I told her you'd return soon tae get her some food. See that she eats something, aye?"

Brody nodded, a satisfied look upon his face as if he thought he had helped Gavin to accomplish some coup—but he supposed the helmsman had.

Cora had resisted him stubbornly about that tunic, though finally she had relented, which gave Gavin some comfort that she wasn't sitting in the cargo well shivering with her lips turning blue. Once again he had tried not to stare at the loveliness of her body when she stripped in front of him, but he was a man after all.

Even thinner than she should be, Cora was fashioned as beautifully as any woman he had ever seen... though it grieved him that seeing her unclothed for the first time hadn't been on their wedding night, he couldn't deny it. He had dreamed of that moment, and to have it so cruelly ripped away from him—och, why was he still torturing himself?

Brody might have said to heed what her eyes were saying when she looked at him, and not her words, but all Gavin had seen was hurt, outrage, and tears. Aye, except for that one moment when she had first lifted her head. He could have sworn he saw a yearning there, a stirring softness, though it had quickly faded when she accused him of lying.

Lying.

Anger had flooded him, but somehow he had kept his composure and told her of his new plan to take her to King Robert—and then she had cut him again by implying that royal favor had won him the surging ship beneath his feet.

Gavin doubted he had ever seen her eyes so wide as when he'd flung open the chest filled with coins. The look upon her face had been even more startled when he said he would offer the gold to the king to free her from her clan.

He had surprised himself, for that matter. Yet how else would he truly learn what lay in her heart if she wasn't given full rein to make up her own mind?

"You dinna look pleased, Laird. I imagine the lass had more unsettling things tae say tae you, but dinna forget—"

"I know, I know, it's all in the eyes." Gavin stood at the railing and looked out across the water, wishing he felt more confident in Brody's advice, even as he remembered how Cora had looked when he told her of his vow to her mother.

Stunned, but confused, too, as if unsure what to think of him—which he supposed meant that he had made some better impression on her after threatening her with a forced marriage. Aye, he could hope.

"Laird, off the starboard side tae the west. A ship—"

"I see it." Gavin had stiffened, his hands gripping the railing as he narrowed his gaze to see more clearly across the waves. "A half league away and under full sail."

"Aye, and heading straight for us from the direction of the island, though it's still too far tae tell if it's Scots or English—"

"Or another raider with a ship much like mine... a birlinn, thirty oars instead of thirty-two and a pitch-black flag atop the mast—*damnation*! We havna seen Ranulf MacDougall's ship for months. Are you ready tae outrun him, Brody?"

9

The helmsman nodded grimly, while Gavin knew then that food for Cora would have to wait.

He needed Brody at his post until they were well away from Ranulf's ship. He didn't fear the raider, och, far from it, but with Cora aboard, Gavin had no intention of engaging him in any confrontation.

The man was as foul-tempered as he was huge, and had bellowed belligerently from his birlinn on several occasions when Gavin and his crew were sailing away from a ship they had raided first, that he was stealing Ranulf's plunder.

Ha! The bastard should be grateful Gavin had sailed south to Normandy for the summer and lessened the competition. Yet why would Ranulf have ventured anywhere near the island? That thought troubled Gavin as he turned to face his crew.

"Oars to water!"

At his roared command, the men scrambled to their benches and thrust the black-stained oars through the oar-holes and heaved with all their might into the task. The ship surged forward with the sleek-ness of a serpent, cutting cleanly through the water while exhilaration swept Gavin.

It was these moments—the wind filling the sail and his men hard at their oars—that thrilled him, he couldn't deny it. The stiff breeze whipping at his hair, he could see that they had already outdistanced the other ship, which made him throw back his head and laugh at the curses Ranulf must be hurling at him.

He had learned the raider's name early on from others of their ilk, but Gavin had kept his own name to himself and demanded that his crewmen not reveal it, either.

Devil of the seas was how he had come to be known, and it suited him well—or at least it had. Now another life beckoned to him of a home to call his own and marriage and children, if Cora's heart wasn't closed to him as she seemed to want him to believe, aye, he prayed that it was so.

"Pull, men, *pull hard!*"

Gavin sat himself down near the prow on the only empty bench and thrust an oar as well through an oar-hole, wrapping his hands firmly around the polished wood.

He had never been a commander to do anything less than what he asked of his men. The rowing exhilarated him even more. . . the muscles in his arms bulging and his lungs filling with the bracing air.

Brody seemed exhilarated, too. He cackled his approval and held fast to the helm, steering the ship through the waves with the expertise of a master. With the crew facing the stern and pulling on oars in tandem and the sail full, Gavin could see in the distance that Ranulf's ship had fallen even further behind.

The bastard would be a fool to follow them to Dumbarton, Gavin was counting upon it.

Raiders were hunted men, no matter that he had never attacked any of King Robert's ships. He didn't know if that was the same for Ranulf, though, and given the man's reputation for cruelty beyond imagining toward those men whose ships he ransacked, Gavin doubted he would dare to dock anywhere near Dumbarton.

Gavin never moored in a port himself, but stayed well to the outskirts or even beyond by several leagues. The traders he dealt with when exchanging his plunder for gold were a shadowy lot and preferred to transact their business well away from prying eyes at bustling wharves.

Yet this time, with Cora aboard, he would risk everything to sail straight into Dumbarton and anchor as close to the castle as he could manage without bringing King Robert's warriors down upon them.

It would be a long night's journey to arrive there by morning, with his men taking turns to get a few hours' rest between stints with the oars. Gavin couldn't afford for them to let up even though Ranulf was so far behind them, which is exactly where he wanted that ruthless raider to remain—*damn him*.

Why had he ventured so close to the island? A remote island so far out of anyone's path that there was no good reason he would have gone there, unless...

Gavin's knuckles grew white from clenching the oar tightly at the unwelcome suspicion that somehow Ranulf had discovered the island's significance to him. . . both as a refuge and that some of his gold was hidden there.

A good thing that storm had erupted or Gavin and his crew might have found themselves engaged in a deadly battle to have come unawares upon Ranulf's ship—though now Gavin found himself wishing that they could turn around and challenge the bastard. Anything to discover why they had sailed a good distance away from the normal shipping routes between England and Scotland.

From his bench, Gavin scanned the straining backs of his men and wished at that moment he could look at their faces.

Had one of them betrayed him? Bitter gall rose in his throat at the unsettling thought, but there was nothing to be done about it right now.

Nor before they reached Dumbarton, for that matter. He needed no disruption that might threaten morale if a hanging must take place—and he needed every single man pulling at the oars to keep them well ahead of Ranulf.

"Row, men—by God, *row*!"

Gritting his teeth, Gavin followed his own command and braced his feet hard against the deck.

Each rotation of the oar told him with increasing certainty that someone among his crew had proved disloyal. Surely if any of the others knew of what had occurred, they would have spoken to Gavin or Brody, who was second-in-command.

Was it one man? Maybe several? His fury growing, Gavin's only consolation was that if Ranulf had found the two chests filled with gold coins, he wouldn't have troubled himself to come after them.

That meant, too, those few monks who inhabited the leeward side of the island hadn't revealed a thing to the raider, but how could they? None of them would have seen when Gavin and his men had buried one chest at the bottom of a cliff under cover of darkness, and another just this past week hidden in a cave well after nightfall.

God help them, Gavin prayed the monks hadn't suffered at Ranulf's hands—which made him glare again at the backs of his men.

A crewman with a pocked face, Farlan MacGinnis, must have felt him staring for he glanced over his shoulder and seemed to gulp, but mayhap that was because Gavin was scowling so fiercely.

Aye, Farlan would be the first one he questioned, he swore to himself, gripping the oars even more tightly as he turned his narrowed gaze to the sea.

MacLachlan Castle
Argyllshire, Scotland

"A MESSENGER, Earl Gabriel, from Rory Campbell!"

Gabriel MacLachlan stood in the half-opened door with his breacan hastily tied around his waist, otherwise he would have stood naked in front of the guard.

Behind him, and shielded from the man's view with his body, Magdalene, his beloved wife, awaited him in their massive four-poster bed.

She was naked, too, and sweetly flushed from their interrupted lovemaking, which made Gabriel curse under his breath.

"M-my apologies, Laird, but the messenger said it was urgent—"

"It's always urgent," Gabriel cut him off, glancing at Magdalene over his shoulder. "Forgive me, my love. I'll return shortly."

He didn't want to leave her at all, she looked so unbelievably fetching with her tousled tawny hair framing her face and her stunning sea green eyes filled with longing.

A longing for him just as he felt for her, their unbridled desire for each other unabated after two and a half months of marriage. They had retired early tonight so they could have more time alone, his duties as the earl of Argyll consuming much of his days.

Yet the evenings, when he wasn't gone from the fortress with his warriors and riding across the countryside in a show of force to deter rebellious MacDougalls, were reserved for his family.

First, supper in the great hall with Magdalene and his two young nieces, Keira and Rhona, and his kinsmen with their wives and children. Then a welcome retreat to the privacy of their bedchamber, which Gabriel reluctantly left behind him as he strode out into the hall.

Barefoot, and still only wearing his breacan, but he didn't care.

He would see this messenger and then return to Magdalene as quickly as he could—though a niggling of intuition told him that Rory's news might not be good.

The chieftain was an ally and a strong one, but mayhap more ambitious than he should be now that Clan Campbell had helped Gabriel, in the name of King Robert, to triumph over the MacDougalls. What trouble might have erupted along the northernmost border of Argyll where they had their stronghold?

Gabriel lunged down the tower steps with the guard trying to catch up; he nearly collided with the dusty messenger, awaiting him at the bottom and flanked by another three guards, their swords drawn.

Though the slight young man with his shock of

coppery hair had come from the Campbells, caution was always the order of the day. Gabriel gestured for his guards to sheathe their weapons after one look at the messenger's anxious face.

"Easy, man, now out with it."

The messenger appeared to gulp as he stared up at Gabriel towering in front of him, and then nodded, finding his voice. "My chieftain, Rory Campbell, sent me tae you because his cousin Lady Cora has fled from our stronghold. He believes she might seek refuge here—or with her kinsmen Cameron or Conall Campbell. Messengers were sent tae them as well—"

"Where is the urgency tae this news?" Gabriel cut him off impatiently. "Of course she's welcome here—"

"F-forgive me for interrupting you, Laird—I mean, Earl Gabriel, but our chieftain wishes her tae be returned straightaway tae the Campbell stronghold. She's tae be married. A northern laird who is most eager tae secure his bride and his alliance with our clan."

"You said Cora fled?"

The messenger seemed to blanch at Gabriel's sharp tone, and bobbed his head.

"Then she mustna be as eager tae wed as this northern laird, aye?"

The young man stared at Gabriel, clearly unsure of what to say, and appeared now to tremble. "M-mayhap... I dinna know..."

"Did Rory appear angry when he bade you tae bring me this news?"

"Aye, furious."

"God help the poor lass. Is she chattel tae be thrust into another unhappy marriage? Since you say she fled, then she doesna want tae marry the man, that's plain enough tae me. If the lady seeks shelter at Mac-

Lachlan Castle, I willna force her back tae Rory, his alliance be damned!"

Gabriel's vehement outburst ringing out around them, he thought the wide-eyed messenger might piss himself from how he'd jumped.

"T-that's not all... not all, Earl Gabriel. Our chieftain believes someone aided her flight... an enemy of our clan. G-Gavin MacLachlan, your cousin—"

"*Gavin?*" Gabriel echoed, astonished. "I havna seen him since we were boys, though he came upon Conall Campbell a week past. The man saved his wife and son—a raider now from the look of things, but what has he tae do with Cora?"

A soft gasp behind him made Gabriel turn to find Magdalene. She appeared to have dressed hurriedly in a rumpled gown, and stood atop the third step, her eyes wide and her hand pressed to her breast.

"Maggie?"

"Oh, Gabriel, canna you see? He must have gone tae rescue her!"

Gabriel gaped at her just as his guards and the messenger, while Magdalene rushed down the steps to his side.

"Aye, it all makes perfect sense! When you and Conall met at Cameron's fortress three days past tae discuss plans for protecting Argyll, Conall couldna say enough about how grateful he was tae the man. So you told me yourself when you returned home, the whole amazing story. Conall's wife, Lisette, deemed the man an angel for rescuing her and little Colin from her hateful sister—och, can you imagine? A raider known as the devil of the seas likened to an angel—"

"Yet this messenger says he's an enemy of Clan Campbell," Gabriel broke in as he wound his arm around Magdalene's waist and drew her against him, and then fixed his gaze once again on the messenger. "Why would that be?"

"H-he thought himself worthy of marrying Lady Cora, but he was only a guard in our chieftain's household and she was already pledged to wed another, Earl Seoras MacDougall."

"There, Gabriel, do you see?" blurted Magdalene, her beautiful face lit with excitement. "It seems Cora hid much from me when we spoke the night you saved King Robert, her own love story. How could Gavin not have gone tae rescue her?"

"Our chieftain believes he wants revenge for being cast out of the stronghold a year ago and forbidden tae return," interjected the messenger. "I was told tae relay tae you that Lady Cora is in terrible danger. Gavin cut down one of our men who confronted him this morning, but he lived long enough to identify his attacker. Mayhap she has escaped from him and will soon find her way tae your gates, Earl Gabriel—but if you say your cousin is a raider, then he has a ship and mayhap took her aboard..."

The messenger grew silent and shook his head gravely, as if anticipating Rory's reaction to this news. Gabriel glanced at Magdalene to see that she had grown sober, too, her fair brow crinkled with concern.

"Ah, God, which one is it?" she murmured, meeting Gabriel's eyes. "Love or vengeance?"

He didn't answer, but already he felt some responsibility for what had happened. He and Gavin were kinsmen after all, and any unlawful act committed by one man reflected upon all of Clan MacLachlan.

"Is there more, man?" he grated, but the messenger shook his head. "Very well, then. Get him some food and take him tae the barracks where he can rest."

As the guards nodded and hustled away the young man, Gabriel tightened his arm around Magdalene's waist and drew her with him up the steps.

"Poor Cora..."

Gabriel nodded at his wife's plaintive sigh for he couldn't have agreed more.

Cameron and Conall's first cousin had suffered grievously while married to Seoras, according to what she had shared with Magdalene, and she couldn't have been more relieved the night he was slain.

Gabriel owed her much as well. If not for Cora crying out for her Campbell clansmen to aid Gabriel and his men in their fight to save King Robert's life, history might have been written far differently for all of them. Yet there was nothing to be done now but wait to see if she appeared at MacLachlan Castle.

God help him, Gavin... with his fire-red hair and fearless spirit, only a few years younger than Gabriel. They had played and rode horses and wrestled together as boys, alongside Cameron and Conall and Finlay MacLachlan, another cousin and Gabriel's most trusted captain. Then Gavin had moved north with his mother after his father's death, and there had been no word of him until now.

An angel or a demon? A rescuer or an abductor? Cameron and Conall already knew that Gavin was a raider, so mayhap they were thinking the very same thing, as Rory's messengers must have already reached them.

If his long-lost cousin was hell-bent upon revenge, Gabriel could only pray that he would bring Cora to no harm.

10

CAMPBELL CASTLE, ARGYLLSHIRE, SCOTLAND

Cameron Campbell strode back to the head table in the great hall, his thoughts troubled by what a messenger from Rory, the chieftain of his clan, had just told him.

His cousin Cora had either fled from the Campbell stronghold far to the north of his own fortress, or she had been abducted... by Gavin MacLachlan.

The same Gavin he had known as a boy and who Conall, his younger brother, and he had rescued from a quaking bog only moments before Gavin would have drowned.

Nothing visible when they had heard him cursing in futility except his head with that fiery red hair, which had thankfully led them to him like a beacon.

Was Cora in danger as the messenger had grimly conveyed? What could be done to save her if Gavin had taken her aboard his raiding ship and was bound for some distant shore? As her kinsman, he was honor bound to do something and so was Conall, who had probably already received the same news.

"Blast and damn," Cameron grated under his

breath as he retook his seat beside Aislinn, his beautiful Irish wife of almost six weeks. Just being near her soothed his dark mood, her vivid sky blue eyes filled with concern as if she sensed his disquiet in spite of the lively commotion in the great hall.

His clansmen were enjoying their supper with great enthusiasm, as they always did, which was in sharp contrast to his unease.

At that moment, he could imagine Cora sitting at this same table beside her husband, Seoras, who had mistreated her so cruelly. Thankfully, those days for Clan Campbell's former overlords, the MacDougalls, were gone. Yet Cameron had every expectation that Gabriel, as the recently appointed earl of Argyll, and Conall, as a newly named baron like himself, would be preventing them from committing further treachery for years to come.

"I will tell you all later, my beloved," he murmured to Aislinn as he squeezed her hand, which felt so wondrously warm in his own.

He needed some time to think of what he must do, aye, mayhap another meeting with Gabriel and his brother, even though they had gathered together only three days ago. He decided, too, that he would send a messenger to Dumbarton to apprise the king of what had happened, though mayhap Gabriel had already done as much. They had been close friends and fought beside each other for so long that it often felt as if they were of one mind—

"Father, I dinna like that boy. He's so. . . so pigheaded! Why must he eat supper with us?"

The indignant voice of his adopted daughter, Sorcha, breaking into his thoughts, Cameron could not help smiling indulgently at her even as he felt warmed that she had called him "Father."

Now Aislinn was "Mother" to her as well, an unexpected gift to them and happening far sooner than they had hoped after the thirteen-year-old had so violently lost her parents only weeks ago. Cameron glanced further down the table to where young David Douglas was heaping his plate with a third helping of roast venison and buttered turnips—or was it his fourth?

The youth wasn't really a boy, either, but fifteen years old and already tall and strapping. His sweaty brown hair was matted to his head and his tunic dusty and disheveled after hours spent on the training field with Cameron's men.

Sorcha surveyed him, too, with an incredulous look on her face—already so lovely for a girl so young, with her striking blond hair and blue eyes—as David shoveled another forkful into his mouth. Some of the food missed its mark and dropped into his lap, but he only shrugged and dug back into his plate, which made Sorcha gasp in dismay.

"Oh, Father, he-he's so—"

"Hungry, from the look of it," Cameron said wryly as Aislinn gave a laugh beside him. "David will be among us for some time, Sorcha, you know his father entrusted him tae me tae train him into a warrior. You might as well think of him as family—a brother, even—"

"That one, *my brother*?" Askance, Sorcha vehemently shook her head. "I've seen better manners among my chickens when I feed them—och, there he goes again!"

Indeed, David was waving over a servant who carried a large platter of roasted meat steaming hot from the kitchen, while Cameron felt grateful for some levity in what had become a marred evening for him.

He didn't know Gavin well enough to guess what he might do if he had vengeance in mind when it came to Cora, and he had become a raider after all—a lawless sort if ever there was one that preyed upon ships for their own gain. Yet as a boy, he had displayed courage and honor and a sense of fair play, and let Cameron not forget that he had saved the lives of Conall's new bride and young son.

Cameron sighed heavily at the disparity, which reminded him of what Conall had said his wife, Lisette, remarked upon. How could a man so merciless one moment be so kind the next?

Would Gavin truly do anything to harm Cora? God help him, if anyone went so far as to steal away his wife or daughter, Cameron knew exactly what he would do... what any battle-honed warrior would do.

He only prayed that wouldn't be the bloody outcome for Gavin, a boyhood friend grown into a ruthless raider... the devil of the seas.

Baron Conall Campbell's Castle
Argyllshire, Scotland

"So you believe Gavin MacLachlan was sailing north to rescue Cora, *oui*?"

Conall nodded, hugging Lisette closer as they lay together in their huge bed. He craved her warmth, her scent, the silken brush of her hair against his skin... everything about her.

His sweet bride of three weeks—God in heaven, how he loved her. He felt again, as if it were yesterday, the scorching pain of thinking he had lost her, and he would have lost her forever if not for Gavin.

The raider had saved Lisette's life and that of his little boy, Colin. His family! No matter what that messenger from Rory Campbell had told him so urgently only moments ago, Conall refused to believe that Gavin meant Cora harm or that he'd taken her out of vengeance.

If they appeared at the gates to his castle, he would welcome them with open arms no matter his allegiance to Clan Campbell.

Yet that occurrence was as unlikely as the moon dropping from the sky. Gavin possessed a sleek, thirty-two-oared ship with a black hull and blood-red sail unlike anything Conall had ever seen. If he had Cora aboard with him, they wouldn't remain anywhere near Scotland, for Gavin must know that Rory wouldn't rest until he found them.

Where might they be bound? France? Ireland? Surely as a raider, he must have plundered enough ships to win him gold aplenty—and he possessed the other half of a sultan's treasure of precious gems as well.

A treasure that his friend of long ago had shared with Conall and Lisette as a wedding gift right before Gavin set ablaze the very ship where Conall's wife and son might have lost their lives. By God, everything in him would have perished that day, too, even if he still lived and breathed!

"He must love her very much to risk his life to steal her away."

Conall gazed at Lisette's lovely upturned face, her soft brown eyes shining in the glow of flames burning in the fireplace.

So he believed as well, and he would send a messenger at dawn to Gabriel and Cameron to tell them of his resolve.

He would do anything he could to help Gavin if the opportunity ever arose... for clearly, Rory Campbell must want him dead.

Why wouldn't he? The chieftain's plans for Cora and an alliance with a northern laird had turned to dust. Wasn't it enough that Rory had already ruined her life once by marrying her off to Seoras MacDougall?

If there was any mercy in heaven, Conall could only pray that his cousin wouldn't succeed in destroying Cora's chance for happiness with a man who had protected *everything* Conall held dear.

"Lisette..." As her slender arms wound around his neck to draw him close, he lowered his head to tenderly kiss his true treasure.

Dumbarton Castle
Dumbartonshire, Scotland

"We're surrounded, Laird, and they dinna look pleased tae see us."

Gavin grunted his agreement to Brody and stared down at the grim-faced warriors who stared right back at him, their shields raised and their swords drawn.

No sooner had they beached the ship against the shoreline than a great hue and cry had gone up that had brought King Robert's men down upon them with astonishing speed.

Their horses snorting and whinnying as the warriors had dismounted into a battle formation three-deep. Gavin had signaled for his exhausted men to remain seated upon their benches or standing with their hands at their sides.

Hands empty of weapons for his crew would be raising none against men ready to protect their king, who Gavin suspected might be watching from a window of the castle nestled at the base of a towering rock.

That intuition gave him some sense of relief that at least King Robert and his men were still quartered in Dumbarton. Yet for how long? It was only an hour past dawn, but already he could see that the windswept bailey was crowded with armed men and packhorses laden with supplies as if they were preparing for an imminent journey.

Gavin hoped they weren't too late for Cora to have her audience with the king. He felt swamped with exhaustion, too, after a long night of rowing with his men, but thankfully Ranulf's ship had given up the chase well before dark.

Gavin focused upon the captain, who sat stiffly upon his mount and eyed him with suspicion. The man was not young nor old, his thick, muscled forearms honed from fighting.

"I am Gavin MacLachlan and this is my ship and my crew. We have raised no weapons against you and havna come tae fight. I have an important personage aboard who wishes tae address King Robert on an urgent matter, Cora Campbell, widow of Earl Seoras MacDougall and first cousin tae Rory Campbell, chieftain of his clan—"

"*Earl Seoras*, did you say?" blurted the man, whose expression had darkened as if Gavin had uttered the very name of Satan himself. "Why would the king wish tae see a woman who shared the bed of the man who sought tae murder him? I was one of the men taken prisoner with him, though the bastards had no knowledge that Robert the Bruce was among us. We were tae be the evening's entertainment and face the executioner's ax right there in the middle of the great hall—"

"And it was *I* that cried out for Clan Campbell tae raise their swords tae help save the king!" Cora admonished him, her outcry piercing the tension in the air as she emerged from the cargo well to stand upon the deck. "I'm first cousin as well tae Cameron and Conall Campbell, one awarded the former MacDougall fortress and the latter a castle of his own for protecting King Robert with their lives. Does our service and loyalty tae the rightful king of Scotland stand for naught in your eyes?"

The captain's eyes had grown wide and he seemed momentarily at a loss for words as everyone stared at Cora, including Gavin.

He had never seen her look more beautiful, her cloak swirling in the breeze over the dark blue gown that had dried and been taken to her earlier by Brody.

Her raven-black hair glossy in the morning sunlight and framing her lovely features as she stood straight and proud and looking every inch her former rank of countess. Sleep and some nourishment had done her a world of good, and though her face was too thin, her cheeks were tinged with a healthy pink that Gavin realized must be indignation.

"So you willna speak tae me, Captain? Very well, I will disembark and *walk* tae the castle so I may address the king—"

"F-forgive me, Lady Cora," the man stammered, dismounting from his horse. "You may ride my steed" —he shot a glare at Gavin—"but the rest of you will remain right where you are."

"*No*, Gavin MacLachlan will accompany me, and your warriors willna harass his crew or step foot upon his ship while we're gone," Cora corrected him, casting a glance at Gavin for the first time since she had left the cargo well.

He caught his breath—how could he not? Her eyes appeared as blue as the deep sea and he would swear her cheeks pinkened further, which made his heart suddenly seem to pound.

He hadn't seen her since he had gone to tell her that he would take her to King Robert—and now they were at Dumbarton Castle, Cora more in control of what had occurred thus far than him. Admiration for her courage and composure swept him as the captain muttered his assent and waved for another two horses to be brought forward, one clearly for himself and the other for Gavin.

"King Robert is addressing the rest of his captains in the great hall," the man added gruffly as Gavin strode toward Cora to assist her from the ship. "I will accompany you there."

Gavin ignored the captain and focused solely upon Cora, extending his hand to her.

To his surprise, she accepted his offer of assistance without hesitation, her fingers trembling in his and as cold as ice. Her lower lip trembled, too, and he realized her audacious display was only a facade to what she really felt inside.

"You were magnificent," he murmured in an aside for her ears alone, to which she met his eyes with such a look of sadness that once again, his breath stilled.

He longed so fiercely in that moment to pull her into his arms and hold her close, but instead he picked her up and settled her gently upon the railing, with her legs over the side. He waved away the two warriors waiting below to assist her, and with one agile movement, jumped from the ship onto the shoreline.

With outstretched arms, Gavin lifted her down as gently, to settle her feet upon the ground, her whole body trembling now as if her courage was flagging. Or was it because he had held her, however briefly? Aye, he could dare to hope.

He took her hand again and led her to the captain's mount, but instead of stepping aside to allow Gavin to assist her, the man encircled Cora's waist with his beefy hands to lift her atop his horse.

White-hot fury shot through Gavin at the captain even touching her, and it was all he could do not to strike the man to the ground. If Cora had noticed his reaction, she gave no sign, but took the proffered reins from the captain and murmured her thanks.

Within another moment, the man and Gavin had both mounted their horses, the phalanx of warriors parting to allow them to pass.

Glancing at Brody, who watched grim-faced from the helm, Gavin didn't like at all that the situation felt entirely out of his control, but the die was cast.

Surprisingly, the captain hadn't ordered him to remove his sword belt, which was one small courtesy for which he could be grateful.

Everything rested now in King Robert's hands, God help them.

Would he intervene on Cora's behalf as she hoped, or send her back straightaway to Rory Campbell and her clan?

11

"Gavin MacLachlan... the devil of the seas. You've made quite a reputation for yourself in a very short time."

Cora gaped in astonishment at Gavin to hear how he'd come to be known—and by King Robert, no less. The sturdily built Scotsman had paid her little heed since she and Gavin had been ushered into an antechamber off the great hall only a moment ago... as if he wanted to assess the strapping Highland raider who stood a full head taller than him and outweighed him in bone and muscle.

Their entrance into the great hall had created quite a stir among the fifteen or so captains standing at attention before the dais where Robert the Bruce had been addressing them.

Everyone had grown silent, including the king, to see Cora and Gavin flanked by six armed guards on either side of them and the stony-faced captain at the lead... but that silence hadn't lasted long. King Robert had roared out for them to be escorted into the antechamber and here they now stood, side by side, while he paced in front of them, all the while never taking his eyes from Gavin.

"I'm sure you're aware that blood-red sail and black hull has marked you far and wide."

"Aye, my lord king."

"My men spotted the distinctive markings a half league away as you sailed down the River Clyde. Some of them have met you upon the high seas. . . and thankfully have lived tae tell the tale."

"Aye, I've not harassed or plundered a single one of your ships, though I canna say that for those belonging to the Scots lairds who oppose you—or their English bedfellows."

That remark drew a gruff laugh from the king, but he didn't stop pacing or studying Gavin. Cora, meanwhile, felt as if she had been entirely forgotten and didn't quite know what to do about it.

She knew King Robert had recognized her at once from the look upon his face in the great hall, and his greeting when he had joined them had been warmly cordial. She had been a part, after all, of saving his life two months ago—just as she'd announced to that captain who had thankfully been dismissed, along with the dozen guards, when they had reached the antechamber.

A spartanly furnished room with a desk beneath a narrow window overlooking the river, the sunlight spilling through and warming away the chill she had felt since lunging out onto the deck of the ship.

She had feared a deadly battle would take place any moment from the captain's belligerent tone, which had spurred her to hasten from the cargo well with the hope that her presence—as a lady—would calm some of the rancor. She knew any mention of her slain husband elicited high emotion; hers, as well. She hated to hear Seoras's name, which only brought back terrible memories that Cora wished she could erase forever from her mind.

Just thinking about him now made her grimace and look down at the floor, which was the same moment that King Robert stopped his pacing to acknowledge her.

"Are you feeling ill, Lady Cora?"

Startled, she met his light brown eyes and felt Gavin's upon her, too, though she didn't glance at him.

"A wee bit, my lord king," she answered him honestly. "I dinna like tae be reminded of the past, but seeing you again today made me think of that night Seoras meant tae kill you. . ." She faltered, sighing. "Forgive me—"

"Och, lass, forgive *me* for leaving you standing there. Here, sit down."

Gratefully, Cora accepted the chair he brought for her, and this time she did glance at Gavin to see that his gaze burned with concern. Looking at him made her tremble anew—how could she not?

The agony in her heart was almost too much for her to bear, to think that soon, they would be parted forever. If Gavin was fortunate, he would never see her again or ever find himself associated with her, no matter her intention to plead for him as well. How else would she protect him from the wrath of her clan? She could imagine Rory's seething rage as soon as he heard from King Robert that Gavin had brought her to Dumbarton, which meant that he had helped her to escape the Campbell stronghold—

"My captain informed me that you wished tae address me about an urgent matter," King Robert's voice broke into her tormented thoughts. "Did you not take refuge with your clan in north Argyll after your husband's downfall?"

"Aye." Cora met the king's gaze, his close scrutiny almost making her falter. "I-I lived at the stronghold with my parents, Owen and Glenis Campbell."

"So I had heard. It may come as a surprise tae you, lass, but I've queried your cousin Rory about your welfare several times in the past few months. Dinna think I have forgotten your courageous outcry that brought your clansmen tae my defense tae fight alongside Gabriel MacLachlan and your cousins Cameron and Conall. Formidable warriors, all three of them,"— King Robert cast a glance at Gavin—"och, it's no wonder they call you devil of the seas with such a one as Gabriel as your cousin. If I've been staring at you, it's that I canna believe how closely you resemble each other—"

"I wouldna know, my lord king," Gavin interjected. "I havna seen him for many years. I was twelve when my mother and I moved north after my father's death."

"Trust my word upon it, you could be near identical from the height and size and look of you, other than your redder hair. Few men stand as tall as Gabriel—aye, or fight as fiercely. Why not command a ship with a blood-red sail, with so fearsome a lineage?"

King Robert gave a laugh again, which made Gavin echo him with the slightest of smiles, making Cora's heart beat faster just to see it. Yet she started in her chair when the king abruptly turned back to her.

"How have you come tae be here with this raider and so far from home?"

"I fled, my lord king," Cora blurted. "I dinna want tae marry the man Rory has chosen for me—"

"Ah, so it's this man you wish tae wed?"

Cora blinked at him, so stunned, she didn't know

what to say. "I. . . yes—I-I mean, *no*! I dinna want tae marry anyone. I'm begging you tae intervene with my clan, please, and spare me from this union. I wish only peace. . . you have a convent near here, aye?"

King Robert nodded, though he had begun to pace again, his expression grown stern.

"You havna told me, Lady Cora, how you came tae be with Gavin MacLachlan. Now answer me!"

"He came looking for me—though I dinna truly know why. He stole into the stronghold early yesterday morning and went tae my house not far from the market. Aye, he even spoke with my parents, but I was already gone and had hidden myself in a wagon. The farmer was leaving the market and heading for the gates. I-I think Gavin spied my shoes and jumped in beside me, God in heaven, I dinna know how he found me!"

"Sometimes fate ordains and sometimes heaven," King Robert said cryptically, stopping to stare at her. "So the devil of the seas brought you all this way so you could speak tae me. What does that tell you, lass? He could have held you for ransom and demanded gold for your release, aye?"

Cora gaped at him, the man's voice so full of authority that she shivered, her composure fled. She only nodded.

"He could have compromised you in some way and treated you ill. You've been aboard his ship since yesterday, aye?"

"Aye, my lord king, but he hasna touched me other than tae help me—though he did speak of vengeance and hatred against my clan and that he would force me tae marry him. *Force me!*"

The moment she said it, Cora felt a stab of regret

and clamped her mouth shut as the king turned upon Gavin, his fists clenched.

"Is this true, MacLachlan?"

Gavin stood with his feet firmly planted and his hands at his side, looking the man straight in the eye. "Aye, in the heat of anger. Our story is a long one and you and your men are clearly preparing tae march, my lord king. Suffice it tae say that I've loved Cora Campbell since the moment I saw her two years ago and hoped tae wed her last year, but my wish was denied me by her clan. She was pledged tae marry another, Seoras MacDougall, and I was deemed not worthy, a fisherman until I became a guard in Rory's great hall. They cast me out of the stronghold and told me never tae return—so my desire for revenge runs deep, I willna deny it."

Gavin stared at Cora now, which made her swallow hard at the pain she glimpsed in his deep brown eyes, until once more, he focused upon King Robert.

"I learned in Dumfries that Seoras had been slain and I knew that Rory would try tae marry her off again. His ambition runs as deep as my thirst for vengeance and one day I *swear*, I will have it."

"Then you are a danger tae my quest tae rule all of Scotland. I need Rory and Clan Campbell on my side and not King Edward's. *Guards!*"

The command was no sooner out of King Robert's mouth than the door slammed open, Cora shrieking and jumping up from her chair. A half dozen warriors rushed into the antechamber, though Gavin kept his hands at his sides and didn't reach for his sword.

Within an instant, he was surrounded and grabbed bodily at his arms and shoulders while King Robert came to Cora's side.

"If you wish him slain, you've only tae command it."

"*Slain*? No! Please, no! I dinna know if he meant his threat, but he did intend tae give you a chest filled with gold if you will only free me forever from my clan. They already forced me into one marriage; I willna survive another. Mayhap if he thwarts the alliance they sought, his desire for vengeance will be satisfied, aye, Gavin?"

She looked at him with pleading in her eyes, but he said nothing. His jaw clenched as if in fury at the men holding him, but still he did not struggle against them.

"You were forced tae marry Earl Seoras?"

Cora's gaze flew back to King Robert, the raw anger in his voice chilling her.

"Aye. Rory insisted I wed him for clan and honor, but it wasna my wish... never my wish."

"Take him out into the hall, but dinna harm him. I wish tae speak tae Lady Cora alone."

Cora could only watch in disbelief, tears burning her eyes, as Gavin was hustled away by the king's warriors, his sword wrested from his belt. He tried to turn his head for a last glance at her, but a rough shove thrust him forward and then the door was shut behind them.

She stood alone in the antechamber with King Robert, who gestured for her to sit back down upon the chair.

Shakily, she obliged him, so close to weeping that she bit her lower lip to try and calm herself. For a long moment, the king said nothing, but went to the window to stare outside until he sighed heavily and turned around to face her.

"You love the man... that much is clear. If not, you

would have allowed me tae cut him down right in front of you for committing such an affront against you. I had tae see for myself what lay in your heart... forgive me for the agony I cost you."

Dumbstruck, Cora could only stare at him, her face burning.

"It's clear as well that you dinna trust what lies in his heart, tae reveal his threat about a forced marriage, though he says he loves you. You've suffered much, Lady Cora, and still suffer. I dinna believe that Gavin MacLachlan would do anything tae hurt you—but as he said, my men are waiting upon me tae march deep into the Highlands. Will you tell me all and spare *me* from having tae demand answers from you?"

Cora nodded, a tiny glimmer of hope flaring within her that she might be able to save Gavin from her clan.

"I love him, it's true. I longed tae marry him, but Rory and his council threatened tae kill Gavin if I didna wed Seoras. So I agreed to the marriage and bid him goodbye... the worst day of my life. Yet more grief was tae come when I received word from my clansmen a week after the wedding that Gavin had died..." Cora faltered, sighing brokenly as fresh tears welled in her eyes. "I wanted tae die... yet it wasna true. He came for me yesterday—out of love or craving vengeance, I canna say. He's not the same. The past year has changed him—"

"None of us are the same, lass," King Robert broke in gently. "How could it be otherwise? Gavin wanted tae marry you and was ridiculed and banished forever from your side. I, too, am separated from my wife, the woman I love. The English hold her prisoner and I dinna know if I will ever see her again."

Cora saw the quiet agony etched in the king's face

and her heart went out to him, but he slowly shook his head as if forcing himself to think of other things.

Her and Gavin, astonishingly.

"I believe it's both that drive him, and only time will tell which one will win over the other. What am I tae do with the two of you?"

"Nothing, my lord king." Cora felt such a terrible ache in her heart that now she could not stop the tears from spilling down her cheeks. "My clansmen swore tae kill Gavin if he ever came near me again. That's why I spurned him yesterday and told him I had never wanted tae marry him—to protect him!"

"Is that when he said he would force you into a marriage?"

"Aye, we canna remain together. We canna marry. . . not if I wish for him tae live. I had hoped a decree from you might turn Rory and the others from their vow, and they would leave Gavin in peace—but I fear nothing can be done. Mayhap they'll hunt him down no matter if I choose life in a convent or return tae marry the man they've chosen for me—"

"I willna send you back to Rory, lass, you have my word upon it. Nor will I send you tae the convent, though the kind sisters there would take good care of you. They sheltered Gabriel MacLachlan's wife, Magdalene, for four years—believing all the while she was a lunatic. . . but of course, you know all of this."

Cora nodded as King Robert gave a wry laugh, and she felt some comfort that he would find humor in so somber a moment.

"Aye, they called her Mad Maggie, but she was no more crazed than you or I—" Cora fell silent abruptly, wondering if she had overstepped her bounds to say such a thing to a king, but he only laughed gruffly again.

"I believe King Edward and his loyal Scots lairds might differ with you—but enough. I will send messengers at once tae Rory that he willna use you again for any alliance or force you into any marriage, upon pain of my replacing him with one of his kinsmen as chieftain of Clan Campbell. Aye, that should quiet his ambition. We'll be marching past his stronghold within the week and I'll reinforce my position, if he has any doubt as tae my resolve. As for Gavin..."

Cora felt her heartbeat seem to stop when King Robert fell silent, as if carefully considering his next words.

"I will demand that Rory and your clansmen renounce any vow tae do him harm... though life is filled with uncertainty, lass. You must seize upon love when it's within your grasp, for you never know when it will be stolen from you." King Robert sighed heavily. "I know this truth well, but you must choose the path your life will take. I only ask that you accept safe shelter until you hear from me that Rory and your clansmen will submit tae my decrees."

"Safe shelter, my lord king? I thought you said you willna send me tae the convent."

"Aye, I'm ordering you and your raider tae sail straightaway tae MacLachlan Castle. Gabriel and his warriors will protect you—and it's time those two cousins meet again. The bond of blood can be strengthened in times of great strife. Now go. My men will escort you back tae the ship where Gavin will rejoin you. I must speak with him first."

"Thank you, King Robert—thank you!" Cora was overwhelmed with such gratitude that she flung her arms around his neck to hug him, but she quickly pulled away, blushing mightily. Yet already he was striding to the door, and flung it open.

Cora hastened after him, her step lighter and her heart racing to see Gavin again as she wiped the tears from her face.

Her raider. Was it possible to hope for such a thing?

She gasped to see him still held fast by the king's warriors, and felt his gaze burning into her back as she was escorted from the great hall.

She could only imagine what King Robert might have to say to him, but she was certain Gavin would be advised vehemently to keep his desire for revenge against Clan Campbell in check. Would he tell Gavin as well that she had admitted her love for him?

Her face burning anew, she prayed that the king would not reveal her true feelings.

Until she heard from him that her clan would honor his decrees, she did not dare to believe that she and Gavin had a chance for happiness. . . though she sent up a fervent prayer that they might—ah, God, please may it be so!

12

"You've a choice tae make, men," Gavin addressed his crew, the bright morning sun warm upon his face. "We will be sailing north tae MacLachlan Castle upon orders from King Robert, but some of you have wives and families tae the south in Ayrshire. You must decide now whether tae take your share of gold, and disembark tae make your way home, or tae remain with me as crewmen aboard my ship. Think upon it, but make your decision quickly for the tide is turning and we must be on our way."

A loud rumble went up from his men, as Gavin had expected for so sudden and momentous an announcement, but the tide appeared to be changing for him, too.

"You must know that our raiding days mayhap are numbered. The king has a need for more ships tae protect the coastal waters of Scotland—and loyal captains tae command them. I have been offered a fleet of fifteen ships being built tae patrol the western coastline, so there's some time yet before my service will begin. Yours as well, if you choose tae stay with me, but there will still be plunder tae share with you, I promise it!"

That pronouncement brought a great whoop from the majority of his men, though seven of them had already stood up. Husbands and fathers each one, which told Gavin he was soon to lose nearly a quarter of his men.

So be it. He had offered them the choice, which was the fair and honorable path. Especially now that King Robert would be testing his allegiance, as the man had made clear in the great hall only a short time ago.

"You must forswear your plans for vengeance against Clan Campbell—or everything I've offered tae you will be withdrawn and I'll be forced tae consider you an enemy. Do you accept this condition, MacLachlan?"

Gavin hadn't considered for more than it took him to voice his agreement... for how else would he have a chance to win Cora if he had nothing to offer her?

No home. No country. No place to raise a family. A life on the sea forever threatened by battles and wind and weather, with her huddled in the cargo well and surrounded by a host of men. That last prospect was too dangerous and far-fetched to consider, and not at all what he hoped one day to provide for Cora.

Even the remote island he had considered a refuge was lost to him if Ranulf MacDougall, and mayhap other raiders, knew now that some of Gavin's gold was hidden there.

It would never be a safe place again for him or his men, let alone Cora—och, he needed the seaside castle in western Argyll that King Robert had promised him if he proved his loyalty and held to his agreement about Clan Campbell.

His gut still burned for revenge, but it was nothing to his intense longing to make Cora his wife—not by forcing her, but with her coming to him willingly.

As his men spoke among themselves, Gavin glanced behind him to where Cora stood in the stern with Brody, the stiff breeze blowing her silken hair around her face.

Such love for her welled inside him that he felt he might burst from it—and he had even proclaimed it in front of her with King Robert as his witness. Yet she had appeared unmoved and still did. . . little changed about her.

Little except how her blue eyes had brightened when he had ridden back down to the ship, followed by a royal messenger, who would accompany them to vouch for Gavin to Gabriel. No warriors guarding him since he and the king had come to an understanding.

Gavin still chafed that those men had held him like a common prisoner, but the thing was done. King Robert had ordered it, and he was grateful they hadn't dragged him down into the Dumbarton Castle dungeon.

The same dungeon where the legendary William Wallace had been held before his journey to London and his execution. Gavin grimaced at the thought of being shoved into a musty cell with his only company the squeaking rats.

He was more than grateful, too, that Cora hadn't wanted him slain on the spot.

The stricken look in her eyes and the horror on her face had reassured Gavin at least that she cared something for him, no matter she had tried to convince him otherwise. Brody had proved right again.

King Robert had told Gavin little of his private conversation with Cora, other than he was sending a messenger to Rory Campbell that she was freed forever by royal decree from her clan's schemes and plans. Gavin had sensed the king wanted to speak to him about something else, but then he must have changed his mind. He had abruptly strode away, no doubt eager to return to preparations for his departure from Dumbarton.

The commotion in the bailey and emanating from the castle was reaching a fever pitch with the shouts of men and squealing of horses, which made Gavin turn back to his crew.

No more of them had stood up, heartening him that he still had enough men to outrow any attackers, which brought Ranulf again to his mind.

Another matter still needed to be addressed, a grim one. Gavin swept his gaze over his men to see if anything stood out to him.

None of them seemed hesitant to make eye contact with him—save for one. The same pock-faced crewman, Farlan MacGinnis, who had glanced behind him at Gavin yesterday and gulped, nervous sweat beading his brow.

Gavin wasn't surprised when Farlan jumped up suddenly from his bench and lunged for the railing, to jump overboard.

"*Seize him!*"

Gavin's command was answered at once by nearby crewmen. As they pulled Farlan away from the railing, he struggled and shrieked as if he knew what was to come. The men dragged him before Gavin and pushed him to his knees.

"Spare me, Laird, please spare me!" he cried out before any query had even been made. "I was drunk and boastful that night, aye, I admit it, but I meant no harm."

"Mayhap, but harm would have come tae all of us if we'd ventured tae the island tae find Ranulf and his men searching for gold—mine and your fellow crewmen's gold! It's enough they gave chase for hours before giving up. By God, man, who did you spill your guts tae about the island?"

"A harlot as drunk as myself—forgive me, Laird! I should have told you, but I feared your wrath...feared *that*—oh, God help me, no... *no!*"

Farlan's frantic eyes widened at the rope with a noose at one end brought forth by Brody; Gavin heard, too, a horrified gasp from Cora, but he ignored it.

Every man upon his ship needed to know the deadly punishment for such an offense, their fellow crewman's cries for mercy desperate... and futile.

"Hang him."

A trio of the burliest men aboard ship stepped forward, the rope flung over the yardarm and the noose dropped around Farlan's neck. He was hoisted high above the deck, his cries choked off and his legs kicking at the air.

Until he kicked no more.

Yet Gavin let him dangle there as even King Robert's warriors, preparing to march out of the bailey, had stopped to stare. Sobbing, Cora rushed past Gavin and disappeared into the cargo well.

He sighed heavily, but such was swift justice upon a raiding ship. Any ship.

Long moments passed before he gave the order for Farlan's body to be cut down. Meantime, he shouted for his men on the starboard side to shove the ship away from the shoreline with their oars. Another full day's journey lay ahead of them to reach MacLachlan Castle, so any serious rest to ease his crew's exhaustion from the night before would have to wait.

First, he planned to drop off those crewmen at the Dumbarton wharves who had decided to return to their families, and then he would arrange the remaining men to make the best use of them. He must parcel out the gold as well, which meant ducking into the cargo well to retrieve the iron-banded chest.

King Robert had mentioned the gold, too, but only that Gavin hold onto it to better outfit the new ships when the time came for him to command them.

As far as he was concerned, the coins didn't belong to him any longer, but to the king and his ongoing fight to rule all of Scotland. Gavin had gotten what he wanted...*freedom* for Cora.

Now he would just have to wait to see what course she chose for her life—and if it mayhap would include him.

A heavy plop into the water told Gavin that Farlan's body had been consigned to the sea. So much for making a better impression upon her... but there had been no help for it. Above all, he demanded unswerving loyalty from his men.

With a resolute sigh, Gavin strode across the deck as his men pulled upon their oars and Brody steered the ship into deeper water.

～

Cora gasped at the sound of determined footfalls approaching the cargo well, which made her lift her head from her knees.

She knew it was Gavin. She sat huddled upon the cot, her cloak wrapped tightly around her. Her eyes burned from crying and her head throbbed, the emotional pendulum of the morning's events proving too much for her.

She should have been happy—elated! King Robert had miraculously agreed to both of her pleas and now she simply had to wait to hear from him that her clansmen had agreed to his demands.

Mayhap it was the uncertainty of it all that had driven her to the edge, along with seeing that dead crewman hanging at the end of a noose.

She had experienced far worse while married to Seoras, when he had forced her to watch executions of prisoners, hapless villagers, and once an eleven-year-old boy who had stolen an ax from the armory. Not to harm anyone, but to cut branches from trees so his widowed mother had fuel to light a fire to warm them.

Her pleas to spare him had elicited only derisive laughter from Seoras—ah, God, the boy had cried out for his life, too...

"Cora?"

She gasped as the heavy canvas fell back into place behind him, leaving them in almost pitch darkness.

"Blast and damn, what happened tae the lantern?"

Cora didn't answer, only listened to him fumbling around for the tinderbox atop a cask.

She hadn't dared to attempt relighting the lantern herself for fear of setting fire to the ship. More low curses followed, but within a moment a warm light filled the space and she saw that Gavin stood right next to the cot.

He looked down at her and she looked up at him, blinking away tears to think of how King Robert could have ended his life with one word—

"Woman, I had no choice but to execute the man. Brody said that you slept so soundly yesterday, you couldna know we were pursued until dark by another raider's ship—Ranulf MacDougall."

"Ranulf?" Cora drew in her breath, realizing that

was the name of the repulsive man who had dined with her and Seoras, the unwashed smell of him making her want to retch. "My husband had a cousin by that name who visited several times at the fortress. . . huge, dark-haired, and with a booming voice—"

"Aye, that's the one. Mayhap it was the lot of them, Ranulf and his crew, but I've never smelled such a stench as when we sailed past his ship after a raid and caught a whiff on the wind."

"Aye, that's the one," Cora echoed, wrinkling her nose in disgust as if she were still sitting at that head table. "Did your crewman know him?"

"No, but the harlot Farlan entertained while we were in Dumfries a week ago went on her way with more than coins in hand. He gave away the location of the island and no doubt that I've gold hidden there—or Ranulf wouldna have bothered to sail that far north."

"The same island where you were going tae take me?" Cora already knew the answer from how Gavin's expression had darkened, and he sighed heavily.

"It's a good thing you didna wish tae go there. We would have had a fierce battle on our hands tae come upon him."

Gavin fell silent and so did Cora, remembering his reaction all too well when she had burst out onto the deck of the ship at the height of the storm. He shut the metal door to the lantern and set the tinderbox upon the cask.

"The hanging was a harsh thing tae see, I'll grant you—"

"I dinna fault you for it, Gavin, I understand. . . and I canna thank you enough for bringing me tae Dumbarton instead."

Her voice had softened, she knew it, Cora staring at him even as he stared back at her.

His face so handsome in the flickering light, his eyes appearing more black than brown and so intense upon her that she felt her heart seem to skip a beat. Flustered, she rushed on.

"Hopefully we'll hear soon from King Robert that my clan will honor his decrees—"

"Decrees? There was more than one?"

Cora blinked, realizing that Gavin knew nothing of her other plea to the king—and not wanting him to know, not yet. What was the use of it? Until she knew that Rory and her clansmen had forsworn their vow to harm Gavin, everything was unchanged between them, it had to be.

"Forgive me, I misspoke. Decree. I owe much tae you, though, and I'll never forget what you've done for me today."

"Aye, I'm grateful, too, that you spared my life. Mayhap you dinna look so unkindly upon me as you claim, Cora Campbell. You heard that I love you. . . and I heard you were forced into your marriage tae Seoras. No clan and honor, but coercion and treachery just as I've always believed. I remember you told me that you would always love me, but yesterday you outdid yourself tae have me think otherwise. *Why?*"

Chapter 13

Cora swallowed hard, her heart pounding so fiercely that she felt it might burst from her breast.

"I dinna know why you're asking me such a thing!" she blurted, panicking. "I've made it plain tae you, Gavin, and I dinna know what else you expect me tae say. Must you torment me? King Robert ordered that we seek safe shelter at MacLachlan Castle until I hear from him, and I canna believe my clan will do anything but agree tae what he demands. Ask me then if you wish, but not today!"

Cora clambered onto the floor to stand facing him, the cot between them, Gavin still looking at her so intently that her knees felt weak.

Why did he have to be so handsome?

Why had her clan threatened to kill the only man she had ever loved?

All she wanted to do was rush into his arms and feel again the stirring warmth of his body—but that would alter nothing. She did not dare surrender to the intense longing threatening to overwhelm her. Her only consolation lay in that King Robert clearly hadn't told Gavin that she loved him, aye, he must have decided that was for her alone to say.

Only when she knew for certain that they wouldn't be forced apart again, never to see each other, never to touch, never to kiss—

"You're trembling."

Gavin's words husky and low, Cora crossed her arms to hug herself tightly as if that would still what she could not hide from him.

"King Robert and I came tae an agreement, Cora. Would you like tae hear it?"

Her cheeks flushing with warmth, she watched wide-eyed as he moved to the foot of the cot, his expression unreadable. Yet his gaze hadn't wavered from her, which made her tremble all the more.

All she could do was nod, the slightest smile stirring his lips.

"I've been appointed the commander of a fleet of fifteen ships he's building, along with a castle by the sea and the title of baron—in exchange for my vow that I willna seek vengeance upon your clan. Does that please you, Lady Cora?"

Her mouth must have dropped open for his smile deepened, though it faded quickly when a shadow passed across his face.

"I will never forgive Rory and your kinsmen for tearing us apart, but relinquishing my plans for revenge seems a small sacrifice if I gain everything I hold dear."

Cora gasped softly at the raw emotion in his voice as he took another step toward her, but then he appeared to reconsider and held his ground.

"*You* have been at the heart of all I've done... becoming a guard tae be closer tae you. Becoming a raider after you were taken from me. I thought you were lost tae me forever until I heard that Seoras had been slain, and then I couldna sail north fast enough tae find you."

"Gavin... please," Cora murmured, her words only making her feel worse, but he shook his head.

"No, Cora, you will hear me. Revenge played no part in my plan tae steal you away from your clan. I knew Rory would try tae marry you off again—I saw firsthand his ambition and heard him speak of his hatred for Seoras, his overlord. Yet he gave you tae that bastard tae strengthen his own power. I knew he would do it again tae forge another alliance, but *no one* was going tae take you from me a second time."

Now Gavin did take a step closer, which made Cora take a step backward, shivering at all he had revealed to her.

"Y-you said hatred spurred you tae find me and that you would force me—"

"Out of anger, just as I told King Robert. When you claimed you never wanted tae marry me—by God, woman! You might as well have torn my heart from my chest, but I dinna believe you. Your words dinna match what I see in your eyes—aye, even now..."

Cora knew it was true as she took another faltering step backward, only to come up against a barrel.

She could go no further.

Her heart hammered as Gavin drew closer, though he did not reach out for her. His expression in the sputtering light was somber, tension tightening his jaw.

"How did Rory force you tae wed Seoras? Did he threaten tae hurt your parents if you refused? Threaten tae hurt you?"

Cora shook her head, though in the next instant she wished desperately she had told him yes, anything to make Gavin cease these relentless questions. The ragged sigh that escaped him made scalding tears blur her eyes, for she knew then that he had guessed the truth.

"So he used me against you, aye? My life in exchange for you agreeing tae the marriage?"

Cora didn't move... didn't utter a word, only the tears coursing down her flushed cheeks giving Gavin his answer.

Slowly, so slowly, he came toward her and drew her into his arms, and she didn't resist him.

Nor did she allow herself to relax, though the strength emanating from him as he tightened his embrace made her want to bury her face against his chest and fiercely hug him back.

How could she? Gavin's realization of how her cousin had coerced her changed nothing.

"If I hadna sworn tae King Robert that I willna seek revenge, I would seek out Rory and cut his throat for what he did tae us."

"No, Gavin, let me go—*please!*"

Cora had stiffened at his words and pushed against him, but still he held her fast and bent his head to press a fervent kiss to her brow. Then he lifted her chin and found her mouth.

The warmth of his lips upon hers sending sweet, aching shivers through her that she hadn't felt since he had last kissed her in the church.

After that terrible day, the only kisses she had known were Seoras's... his mouth crushing painfully down upon hers, his wine-soaked breath and the smell of his rotten tooth making her gag—

"*God help me, noooo!*" Cora pushed harder against Gavin this time, her balled fists beating at his chest. "*Let me go... you must let me go!*"

He did, stepping back though he still held her hands, but she wrenched them away.

"Cora... what the devil?"

She spun around so that her back was to him, her spine rigid, her breathing ragged as she tried in futility to compose herself.

"Please, Gavin, leave me. We've nothing more tae say tae each other... not right now, I beg you!"

She didn't know if it was the desperation in her voice or her pleading with him that made him oblige her, but his muted curse and heavy footfalls told her that he had retreated.

She heard a scraping upon the floor, and then a grunt from Gavin as if he had picked up something heavy. Then he was gone, sunlight bursting into the cargo well for an instant before the canvas closed behind him.

Only then did Cora fully break down and collapse sobbing upon the cot.

A terrible realization hitting her that it wasn't just

her overwhelming fear for Gavin that had made her spurn him... but that she couldn't bear the intimacy of his touch.

Seoras had ruined her! She began to weep all the harder, pressing her hand over her mouth so the sound wouldn't carry outside.

Even if King Robert sent word that Rory had agreed to his decrees—freeing her from her clan and Gavin from the death sentence they had laid upon him, how could she and Gavin remain together if his kisses only brought forth sickening memories of Seoras?

Cora buried her face into the cot and sobbed inconsolably... the prospect of the rest of her life spent in a convent looming even closer.

~

"Is aught amiss, Laird?"

Gavin scowled at Brody, the helmsman's matter-of-fact query more a statement that there was no need for him to answer. He slammed shut the lid to the chest and watched as his seven crewmen disembarked from the ship docked at one of Dumbarton's busy wharves, most likely never to return.

Why would they with gold in their pockets and their wives and families waiting for them? He had given the men more than their due, but they had earned every coin. He had scarcely uttered a word to them, the muffled weeping from the cargo well making them shift their feet uncomfortably and appear most eager to be on their way.

Gavin was eager, too, to be gone from this town and out on the water again where the whistling wind would mask Cora's sobbing.

God help him, when had any man been blessed to understand a woman? *Never*, as far as he knew, that hard cold fact making him rise from the bench and lift up the chest that seemed not much lighter for the gold coins he had doled out to his men.

"She'll only cry the harder if you go back there again," Brody said dryly as Gavin's dark look at his remaining crew made them all scramble to take their seats and ready the oars to shove off from the wharf. "Best tae leave the chest outside for a wee bit and give her some time tae fall asleep. . . or at least tae settle herself. What did you say tae her tae bring on such a flood?"

Gavin didn't answer, but dropped the chest at the entrance to the cargo well and then strode to the stern, Brody following him. To a man, everyone in his crew stared at him as if waiting for his commands—or mayhap they were curious, too, to hear his answer to his helmsman's query.

He didn't give any of them the satisfaction. Instead, he gestured to one crewman after another to reorganize them upon the benches until he was certain they were all seated where they were needed to effectively man the ship. Brody stood silently at the helm, Gavin scowling again to feel the weight of the man's gaze upon him.

"Push away from the dock!"

The scraping of oars eased the worst of his darkened mood for soon they would be back out in deep water and heading north.

As his crew put their backs into the task and rowed away from the wharf, Gavin turned to Brody to find him concentrating on steering the ship out of the way of other ships and small fishing boats. That small act of mercy would at least keep the helmsman from asking him any more pointed questions... for a time.

Gavin, meanwhile, focused upon issuing commands, the sail soon hoisted and filling with wind, a good sign for the journey.

He had never ventured close before to MacLachlan Castle, situated at the eastern end of a narrow sea loch, or so King Robert had told him, which was another boon. His ship would have no trouble navigating those waters to reach their destination—but arriving there safely was another matter.

Gavin had no doubt that Ranulf lurked somewhere along the way, which made him cast a glance over his smaller crew. Less men in a battle might make a difference, but there was no help for it now—

"Baron MacLachlan, I would speak with you."

Gavin glanced at the owlish-looking messenger who had approached him. Taken somewhat aback to be addressed as a baron, he could see that Brody appeared surprised, too. The older fellow with his big round eyes and thin, wispy hair appeared more a scribe than one to brave countless dangers to deliver royal messages, but he had handled his horse with great skill while riding with Gavin from the castle to the ship.

"Your name?"

"Ivor, Baron. Ivor MacPherson, and honored tae be aboard your ship. King Robert was highly impressed with you tae have come so far and so fast as a raider, and he expects great things from you as the commander of his western fleet. There are two of your ships now tae accompany us tae MacLachlan Castle."

Gavin was a man rarely astonished by anything, but seeing the thirty-six-oared birlinns cutting through the water toward them left him momentarily speechless.

The king's flag, emblazoned with a golden lion, fluttering proudly from the top of each mast and with full crews manning the ships—by God, both of them even larger than his own!

"Your flag, Baron."

Gavin accepted the wrapped bundle from Ivor and hastily opened it, the gravity of the moment not lost upon him. He strode at once to the mast to pull down his own flag—blood-red with a black, coiled serpent at the center—and replace it with King Robert's banner, a sense of great responsibility settling over him.

Aye, his life had taken a new course and he would do everything in his power to merit the king's trust in him, Gavin wishing Cora was standing beside him to witness such an important moment. Was she still sobbing in the cargo well?

Anger at himself suddenly swept him that he might have done anything to grieve her. He had hoped telling her that he no longer sought revenge against her clan would please her, and she had appeared astonished by his news.

Yet when he had started to come toward her, she had begun to look desperate, backing away from him even as he spilled out his heart to her.

Just as he had long suspected, her clansmen had forced her into an unwanted marriage by threatening his life... but Gavin sensed there was more to it than what she had revealed to him with her tears.

God help him, she had wed another man to save his life, which meant that she must truly love him. Was she somehow protecting him still, to reject him at every turn since she first came aboard his ship? To strike him moments ago with her balled fists when he had pressed his lips to hers. . . just as she had screamed at him when she had awoken yesterday to find him kissing her?

Kissing her...

"You're a fool, MacLachlan. . . a blind fool." Gavin's fury with himself increasing as Brody's cautioning words flew back to him about what Cora had suffered as Seoras's wife, he turned from the mast to find that Ivor stood right behind him. "*What is it, man?*" he demanded, venting some of his spleen upon the messenger, who backed up several steps.

"Baron, King Robert wishes you tae take up residence at the castle he has provided for you as soon as word comes of Clan Campbell's submission tae his decrees. You'll find a fine harbor for your ships and warriors are already quartered there who will answer tae your command."

Decrees? There it was again, Gavin looking at Ivor with irritation and registering little else of what the man had said. "Is it more than one decree?"

"Aye, two, and messengers are already riding north tae deliver them within a few days tae Rory Campbell. The king always sends more than one man in case of any mishaps. The first decree releases Lady Cora from any further obligations tae her clan so she may conduct her life as she chooses—and the second regards you, Baron. King Robert demands that the Campbells renounce the vow they made to kill you if you ever went near her again, especially now that you hold such an important status as one of his commanders."

"So that's it," Gavin said under his breath, his fury stoked again that the Campbells still wished him dead.

Cora's agreement to wed Seoras had gotten him alive out of the stronghold that day, but Rory's men had come looking for him the next morning—no doubt intending to murder him.

His death would have put the matter to rest once and for all, as far as Rory was concerned, but fate had taken an unexpected turn with Seoras slain and Cora a widow. The last thing the chieftain would want was Gavin coming into her life again to thwart him, just as Gavin had done, and Cora must know it—och, so she *was* still protecting him!

His heart pounding, Gavin wanted nothing more than to return to the cargo well, but his new duties demanded his attention with the two ships in full sail behind them.

Aye, and let him not forget that it wasn't just the one matter at the heart of Cora spurning him. Like the decrees, there were *two*—the second one making him wish fiercely again that he would have been the one to lop Seoras's head from his body.

There may be no marks upon her skin, but in her mind, her heart? Och, I wouldna be surprised if she doesna wish for a man tae touch her ever again...

So Brody had warned him before Gavin had even ventured into the stronghold to find Cora—and those words haunted him now as to what she must have thought of his kisses.

Not filled with love and longing... but forced upon her just as her marriage had been forced upon her, Gavin feeling sickened and infuriated by the cruelty she must have endured at Seoras's hands.

At the misery *Gavin* had made her suffer to have threatened to wed her against her will.

His beloved Cora.

God help him find a way to ease the painful memories of whatever had happened in the past so she would open her arms and her heart to him. . . aye, please may it be so.

~

"I SEE THREE SHIPS, Laird. Gavin MacLachlan's in the center and two birlinns sailing behind—and all are flying King Robert's flag."

"Blast him!" Infuriated, Ranulf peered as well into the distance to see exactly what his sharp-eyed crewman had revealed to him. "What madness is this? Is he no more a raider, but become one of that false king's men?"

The crewman didn't answer, but wiped away the spittle from his face that Ranulf had spewed upon him in his fury.

Meanwhile, Ranulf pounded his huge fists upon the railing in frustration.

What was he to do now? By God, he wanted that gold and he would have it! Chasing after one ship to attack was no great task for him—but three? Top-of-the-line ships, too, he could see now as they drew closer—and even larger than Gavin's, with thirty-six oars apiece.

Hidden from the main waterway in this protected inlet, Ranulf had no fear that his own ship would be seen. . . and clearly, there was only one thing he could do.

Follow them at a distance and determine where they were bound—mayhap if he was lucky, to the island. He and his men could then come upon them at night and eliminate all three crews one by one with stealth and cunning and the silence of their knives, leaving only Gavin alive to lead him to the gold.

His damned gold! Ranulf could almost feel the

coins sifting through his fingers when he dug his hands into those chests, anticipation swelling inside him.

That arrogant devil of the seas would soon find himself a corpse sinking into its murky depths if Ranulf had anything to say about it, aye, he couldn't wait!

13

"Oh, Cora, I canna believe you're here! I'm so glad King Robert sent you tae us for safe shelter."

Cora summoned a weary smile for Magdalene, the young woman as vivacious and lovely as she remembered from two months ago. . . while she must look dispirited and pale in comparison.

How could she not? Heavy of heart and exhausted from a restless night aboard Gavin's ship, Cora felt as if the mid-afternoon sunshine streaming into the bedchamber where she had been ushered was mocking her.

"He's so handsome, Cora, your Gavin MacLachlan —and did you see how much he and Gabriel resemble each other? It's astonishing! They're cousins for certain, but they look like brothers. I could tell Gavin wanted tae assist you up the tower steps, but my husband wouldna hear of it, I'm afraid. They have much tae discuss, aye?"

"He's not my Gavin," Cora murmured, but her words went unheeded from the bustle of activity filling the well-appointed room.

Logs blazed in the fireplace with its finely carved

mantel, colorful tapestries graced the walls to hold in the warmth, and a thick rug covered much of the floor. The furniture was intricately carved as well, a luxurious brocade spread in hues of blue and violet and gold gracing the wide bed with its matching canopy.

She had heard Seoras scoff at the riches Gabriel's elder brother, Malcolm, had spent on fine clothing and furnishings, which had led to his financial downfall and death—God rest him, a foul murder committed by one of Seoras's henchmen.

That unfortunate extravagance had led Gabriel, after he inherited MacLachlan Castle with its empty coffers, to appeal to Seoras for gold so he could feed the hungry people under his charge and make repairs long neglected. Aye, much needed coin Gabriel obtained only after agreeing, reluctantly, to take Mad Maggie for his bride.

Yet Magdalene had never been a lunatic at all, but so winsome and good-hearted a lass that grateful tears filled Cora's eyes as a copper tub was carried into the room, accompanied by a host of servants bearing steaming buckets of water.

Ah, God, a bath. Gavin's helmsman, Brody, had done the best he could by offering her a bucket of cold seawater with which to bathe herself, though the salt that lingered still chafed her skin.

Yet she had thanked him warmly, Brody the only one to venture into the cargo well since they had left Dumbarton late yesterday morning.

He had made sure she was warm enough and had food to eat and that the lantern was always lit for her —making Cora remember when Gavin had fumbled in the near darkness for the tinderbox.

Making her remember, too, as Magdalene gave directions to the servants, the moment when he realized she had married Seoras to save Gavin's life...

"Och, Cora, you've gone as white as a sheet! Have you eaten today?"

The alarm in Magdalene's voice reviving her, if only a little, she nodded—but already her former sister-in-law was calling for servants to bring up hot food and drink as quickly as they could.

"Here, now, let's get you undressed. Surely a bath will make you feel better."

Magdalene had no sooner gestured to the maidservants remaining in the room than Cora was helped out of her clothing with practiced efficiency. She wasn't surprised, a few moments later, to find herself settled into the tub placed in front of the fireplace.

The wondrous warmth of the lavender-scented water soothed her at once, a soft sigh escaping her.

Magdalene smiled and plopped down in a chair, but she immediately jumped up with a look of apology on her face.

"Surely you wish tae bathe alone—"

"No, no, stay with me," Cora insisted gently. She sighed again as one of the maidservants knelt behind her to run a sudsy sponge across her shoulders and upper back. Another young woman lifted her right arm to do the same, making Cora feel as pampered as a queen though she usually tended to her own needs.

Even when she had been a countess, she had bathed and dressed herself, but that had been more to prevent her servants from seeing the marks and bruises upon her body from Seoras's degrading ill-treatment—

"Is the water too hot? Now you're as red as can be," blurted Magdalene at the sudden firing of Cora's cheeks.

"It's fine. . . truly." Some of her enjoyment had faded at the unwelcome memories, but she didn't want to distress Magdalene, who was being so solicitous of her. Cora made herself relax and lean her head back as one of the maidservants slowly poured a pitcher of warm water on her hair to wet it for washing.

"Aye, that's good," came Magdalene's approving voice as Cora closed her eyes at the comforting sensation of fingers massaging her scalp. "I'll see that your gown and cloak are cleaned—your slippers as well. I have gowns aplenty tae share and we're close tae the same size, though you're a wee bit taller than me. I'm sure you didna take much with you, if anything, when you fled your clan's stronghold—och, Cora, forgive me. I should have waited tae say anything. . ."

Cora had opened her eyes and abruptly sat up, splashing water onto the floor. "You know what happened?"

Magdalene's quick nod made her heave a sigh, for there had been no time to offer any explanations when she and Gavin had been escorted into the massive keep by Gabriel MacLachlan.

A fearsome-looking man, he and a host of armed warriors had met Gavin's ships when they anchored along the shoreline of the loch—aye, Brody had told her that they had two new birlinns accompanying them from Dumbarton, all three flying King Robert's flag.

Cora had only emerged from the cargo well moments before, and Gavin had said nothing to her, though she had felt his gaze following her when she went to stand by the railing. He and the royal messenger had disembarked together and gone to speak to Gabriel, who appeared to relax his grim-faced posture after hearing what the two of them had to say.

Then she had disembarked with Gavin reaching up to lift her down, the strength of his hands encircling her waist sending shivers through her.

Yet she felt so awkward toward him after she had spurned him once again, and he had seemed stiff and almost as forbidding as Gabriel had looked at first. Horses were brought forward for them, Cora riding silently beside Gavin to MacLachlan Castle, which could be seen from the loch, along with a good-sized village that lay to the east.

An imposing keep with four square towers was surrounded by ramparts, the castle not as big as the fortress where she had lived with Seoras, but impressive all the same. A moat filled with sharp-sided boulders surrounded the outer walls, and they had ridden across a drawbridge and beneath two raised iron gates to gain entrance to the bailey.

It was clear why King Robert had deemed Gabriel's castle a safe shelter, a striking number of warriors manning the ramparts and training strenuously with swords and shields at the center of the bailey, in addition to the men that had accompanied him to the loch.

Other than an invitation to follow him, Gabriel had said little else as he led her, Gavin, and the royal messenger into the keep—where Cora had stumbled, she knew not if from the exhaustion she felt after so little sleep or that Gavin still looked as stiff-shouldered and grim as before.

Yet he had caught her arm at once to prevent her from falling. His grip strong and his gaze intense upon her, while Magdalene, awaiting them at the entrance to the great hall, had cried out in alarm.

"Cora, are you all right?"

"Take her upstairs, Maggie, where your maidservants can tend tae her," Gabriel had cut in before Cora could utter a word. "Gavin, you will accompany me."

With Gabriel's stern tone brooking no argument, Cora had nonetheless felt Gavin's hand linger at her arm as if he was reluctant to leave her.

"*Baron MacLachlan.*"

Gabriel's tone grown brusque with impatience, Gavin had uttered a curse and released her while Magdalene had rushed to her side to walk with her up the tower steps to the third floor.

Now Cora sat in a tub of water growing tepid while her tawny-haired hostess signaled for a final rinse of her hair and hastened herself to an armoire to pull out a robe.

"A messenger arrived two days ago from Rory Campbell tae tell us you had fled and tae watch out for you in case you made your way here," came Magdalene's explanation as she returned to the tub. "He wants you returned straightaway tae your clansmen, but Gabriel told the man if you sought refuge with us, he wouldna send you back."

"Thank God," Cora murmured, her hand rigid upon the rim as she stood up, dripping wet, though she was quickly enveloped in the soft robe. Yet not quickly enough to stop Magdalene from gasping, her stunning green eyes grown wide.

"Cora... that scar upon your left hip. I-it looks like teeth marks... as if someone bit you."

A sick feeling rising inside her, Cora accepted the assistance from a maidservant as she stepped out of the tub. "My husband... Seoras. Please, I dinna wish tae speak of it—"

"Oh, Cora... forgive me." Her face bright red, Magdalene gestured for chairs to be brought close to the fire even as another serving maid entered with a tray laden with food. "Here, come and sit with me."

Cora nodded and obliged her, though her fingers trembled at the memory of the worst night of her marriage. Her wedding night—ah, God, help her one day to forget.

She took her seat across from Magdalene while a small table was brought for the tray, though nothing upon it—fresh-baked oatcakes and a steamy bowl of soup—looked like anything Cora could eat for how nauseous she now felt.

"What else did the messenger say?" she said with trepidation, almost wishing she hadn't asked. Magdalene still appeared stunned by what she had seen, her voice grown subdued.

"He mentioned the planned marriage. . . a northern laird and an alliance with your clan. Gabriel told him you couldna have wanted such a union tae have fled—"

"Aye, it's true."

"So we believed, too, and then the man said you had been aided by an enemy of your clan, Gavin MacLachlan."

"*He did?*" Cora blurted, stunned. "How could they have known?"

"Och, the man he struck down. He lived long enough to name him. Your clansmen think Gavin seeks revenge against them and that you're in terrible danger—but it canna be so, Cora! Even for those few moments downstairs, I saw how he looks at you. He canna mean you harm, I would swear tae it. Gavin saved the life of Conall's wife and his little son—aye, on his way north tae find you. He may be known as the devil of the seas, but Lisette believes him an angel for rescuing her, and so do I! I saw how *you* looked at him, Cora, you must love him—"

"*I canna allow myself tae love him!*" Tears welling in her eyes, Cora tried to compose herself by looking into the sputtering fire, but it was no use. She met Magdalene's gaze again, not surprised to find her appearing as stunned as Cora had felt moments ago. The maidservants looked startled, too, standing stock-still and wide-eyed as if waiting for whatever she might say next.

"Please, Maggie... I will tell you all, but we must be alone."

"Aye, of course... *of course!*" With a simple, "Leave us," Magdalene had the room emptied, the door closing with a thud behind the maidservants as she fixed her eyes with great compassion upon Cora. "Go on..."

∽

"So we must wait for word from Rory that he's accepted King Robert's decrees."

"Aye," Gavin murmured, staring into the face of a man who could very well pass for his own brother. Gabriel looked hard at him as well, and laughed under his breath as he shook his head.

"Gavin, by God. You were a skinny lad when last I saw you, but look at you now. Strapping and tall—aye, we can look at each other eye tae eye and that's a rare thing, only Cameron coming as close tae me in height. Och, well, Conall's not far behind him... and speaking of the man, he's as grateful tae you as anyone could be for saving his family. We're *all* grateful tae you— though if it was vengeance that made you steal Cora away, we would have tae trade our appreciation for swords. Like King Robert, we need the Campbell clan's help tae keep peace in Argyll. Tell me again you understand that we've no patience for any plans for revenge, aye?"

"Aye, I understand. Just as I told you and the king, I swear tae it."

"Good. I'll send messengers tae Cameron and Conall so they know you didna abduct their cousin—och, Conall didna believe it of you, either way. Like me, Cameron hoped it wasna true, so he'll be glad of this news."

Sensing that Gabriel was just as glad, Gavin leaned back in his chair and took another draught of ale.

He wasn't a man fond of drinking, but the frothy stuff tasted good as he allowed himself to relax, an air of conviviality between him and Gabriel that he hadn't experienced in a very long time.

As boys, their adventures had been many, and speaking as well of Cameron and Conall had brought back fond memories of days gone by.

Well, except for when Gavin had nearly drowned in that stinking bog, the Campbell brothers coming to his rescue in the nick of time. He gave a low laugh while Gabriel, seated opposite him, drank from his own refilled cup.

With a blazing fire in the massive hearth warming Gavin, his belly full from a hot meal he had wolfed down and the ale chasing it, he felt a few moments' peace, which for him, was all too rare.

He glanced at Gabriel to find his cousin had lowered his cup to study him, not in any dark way, but with an honest query in his brown eyes that so matched the color of Gavin's own.

"So... will you be marrying the lass?"

Gavin's cup froze midway to the arm of his chair,

and he was glad at that moment he had no ale in his mouth for he might have spat it out in surprise.

Yet in the next instant, his hand tightened as tension filled him, a sudden change of demeanor that he knew Gabriel had noted.

"If Cora will ever have me." Gavin sighed heavily, and looked into the fire. "She's spurned me at every turn since I brought her aboard my ship, but at least now I know why—or I think I do. Who can say? Women are such a puzzlement."

Now it was Gabriel who appeared startled, though in the next instant he threw back his head and gave a roar halfway between laughter and sheer incredulity.

"Do you know what my wife was doing the first time I saw her? Running naked across a convent courtyard tae jump into a fountain! She was feigning lunacy, and I'm ashamed tae say it took me a damned long time tae realize she wasna mad at all. There's really no making sense of them until they *want* you tae make sense of them—by God, man, do you have the stomach for it? It's a hard-fought battle, but the rewards..."

Now Gabriel stared into the fire, no doubt thinking about Magdalene, while Gavin's thoughts had never left Cora—no matter everything his cousin had wanted to discuss with him.

Was she thinking about him? Mayhap sleeping, given how exhausted she had looked with those gray smudges beneath her eyes? Gavin had wanted to go to her a hundred times aboard ship, but had held back the entire journey to MacLachlan Castle, not wanting to distress her further or cause another flood of tears.

He didn't know what to do or what to say... the dilemma of it all making him take another long draft of ale.

"You love her, Gavin, that's plain. Are you going tae surrender tae the impossibility of it all, or will you show the lass that you're the only man for her no matter the obstacles you face? Aye, especially the ones plaguing her mind and her heart—God help you, those are the worst, I dinna envy you the task."

Gavin, nearly having choked upon his ale, felt certain that his cousin was one of the wisest men in Scotland as Gabriel raised his cup to him.

"The rewards, man. . . *never* lose sight of the rewards."

14

"Will Lady Cora come down for supper, Mama?"

"Mayhap if she managed tae get some rest—but if she doesna join us, we'll see her in the morning."

A girlish sigh of disappointment from Keira, Gabriel's six-year-old niece, greeted Magdalene's words, while Gavin felt like heaving a sigh, too.

One filled with fresh exasperation at himself that he hadn't spoken to Cora since she had demanded tearfully he leave the cargo well—och, but they weren't aboard his ship any longer, the great hall bursting with Gabriel's clansmen and their families gathered for the evening meal.

Gavin's crew was there as well, along with the men who had manned the other two birlinns, all three ships heaved up onto the shoreline and well-guarded by some of Gabriel's warriors.

Fortunately his cousin had a huge barracks to house them all until they set out for the castle King Robert had granted to him, but when might that be? Gavin's gaze flew back to the entrance to the hall as

Gabriel's sage words of reassurance echoed in his head.

The rewards, man... never lose sight of the rewards.

The greatest reward Gavin could think of was hearing from Cora's lips that she loved him, but who could say when—or *if*—that might be, either?

"Baron MacLachlan, dinna you like your supper?" queried Keira while her younger sister, Rhona, dug a spoon with gusto into her bowl.

"Umm, I love stew!" pronounced the four-year-old, her plump cheeks smeared with brown gravy.

Gavin knew from Gabriel about the tragic demise of the girls' parents within the last two years, but thankfully they looked happy, with their sparkling blue eyes and dark curls. It seemed to please Gabriel and Magdalene immensely that the youngsters called them Papa and Mama, which made Gavin yearn for bairns of his own one day, he couldn't deny it.

Just to please the girls, he dug into his own bowl and popped a huge mouthful of venison stew into his mouth and chewed with exaggeration—which made them erupt in giggles.

"Och, dinna choke, man," came Gabriel's wry remark while Magdalene laughed, too, though she sobered to stare at him thoughtfully.

All of them were seated at a trestle table and not upon any formal dais, with one chair still left open for Cora, if she chose to join them. Again, Gavin's gaze flew to the entrance and he felt the same sense of vexation at himself, along with no small amount of impatience.

How would he ever have a chance to ease any pain he had caused her these past few days if she refused to come down and preferred to stay in her bedchamber?

"May I have some more stew, Mama?" piped up Rhona, having emptied her bowl. "Please?"

"Patience, sweetheart, patience," Magdalene murmured, doling out a couple generous spoonfuls from her own bowl as she glanced at Gavin with a soft smile. "A wonderful virtue for not only bairns tae learn, aye?"

Clearly, she spoke to him, which made Gavin force himself to relax and focus again on his meal, though he really tasted little.

He missed seeing Cora. He had no wind and weather and the duties of commanding a ship to occupy his mind or help to rein in the intense longing that threatened to overwhelm him. Mayhap he should just excuse himself from the table and take a vigorous walk around the bailey—

"Look, it's Lady Cora!" announced Keira while Rhona twisted around on the bench.

"Oh, she's so pretty, aye, Mama?"

As Magdalene murmured her assent, Gavin felt as if his heart had lurched against his chest. He turned around, too, and saw that Cora walked slowly toward the entrance from the direction of the tower where she had disappeared earlier.

She moved so slowly in fact, that he wondered if she might be thinking to turn around and retreat back upstairs.

"Go on, man," came Gabriel's low voice. "Before someone else jumps up tae accompany her—och, there you go."

Indeed, a burly, dark-haired warrior had stood up from his bench, but Gavin lunging to his feet seemed to make many gasp around him.

Or mayhap it was his dark look of warning that

made the man sit down and no others rise in his place. . . while Gavin strode toward the entrance.

"Ah, God. . ."

Cora had whispered to herself, her heart racing to see Gavin rise so abruptly to wend his way around trestle tables and benches filled with men, women, and children looking at him.

Looking at her.

Nervously, she smoothed the skirt of her sapphire-blue gown and tried her best to focus upon what Magdalene had said to her. . . the first words in days that had truly soothed her heart.

She had revealed everything, spurred by Magdalene's quiet empathy and that her former sister-in-law had held her hand as tears fell from both of them, punctuated by sighs and heartfelt reassurances.

"I canna fault you for how you feel, Cora, after all you've suffered. I, too, was afraid tae give Gabriel my heart, though your reasons are different than mine. I didna trust him or love him—but everything changed and I canna imagine my life without him. Yet he's a warrior, just as Gavin is a warrior, and danger will always be near. We canna protect them from harm no more than we can catch sunlight between our fingers. . . but we can love, Cora, with every breath, every kiss, every embrace. I would rather know one day, even one hour with Gabriel than never tae have loved him. . ."

Cora swallowed hard as emotion tightened her throat, but somehow she lifted her chin as Gavin drew closer. In the light cast by blazing torches, had she ever seen him look more handsome?

His forest green tunic, mayhap one of Gabriel's, fit

his powerful body snugly, and his dark red hair was still damp as if freshly washed, and loose around his shoulders. She found herself thinking she preferred it that way, wild and unfettered like the man, which made her face grow warm. Yet it was his gaze riveted upon her that made her heart begin to pound.

"Cora..."

His voice low and intense, she could see the longing in his eyes that so matched what she felt enveloping her, rooting her to the floor.

He had held out his hand to her, but she stared at it almost stupidly, as if in a daze—aye, she didn't feel at all like herself anymore.

Where had her resolve flown to spurn him until she heard from King Robert? She should have stayed upstairs! She should have locked herself in her room and not come out until a royal messenger arrived at MacLachlan Castle.

Magdalene's words had soothed her enough to make her dress and venture from the tower, but seeing Gavin again was a stark reminder that nothing had changed, nor could change, until she knew if her clan had accepted the king's decrees... no matter how much she wished otherwise—

"Cora, whatever you're thinking... whatever you're feeling, dinna turn from me and run back tae your room, I beg you."

The husky plea in his voice making her face burn even hotter, Cora knew he had sensed her panic even as he took her hand, his strong fingers warm and reassuring.

"Come into the hall with me. Gabriel and Maggie and their girls are waiting for you—och, you must be hungry."

"I'm not hungry. I ate earlier... some soup and oatcakes. I-I dinna know why I came down, it was a mistake—"

"It's no mistake tae be among those that care about you, lass, but you dinna have tae go into supper if you dinna wish it. Would some fresh air tempt you? Come walk with me, it'll do us both some good."

Gavin closed the distance between them to stand next to her, Cora's hand still clasped in his, though he didn't attempt to steer her toward the arched doorway that led outside.

Instead he waited patiently for what, to Cora, felt like an eternity as she stared into the great hall at the faces turned toward them, everyone watching with curiosity, and then looked back to Gavin—finally nodding at him.

"Good, it's a fine night and a rare thing for me tae find myself aground. Now if the floor will only stop rocking—"

"Truly?" she blurted, for she felt a wee bit of that same sensation as if she were still aboard ship. His teasing smile made her gasp, and she smiled back at him before she even realized what she was doing.

If Gavin noticed, he gave no sign of it other than a slight tightening of his fingers, and led her to the doorway while Cora walked alongside him with no hesitation.

She couldn't deny it, his suggestion of fresh air sounded wonderful to her... anything to cool her flushed cheeks.

Other than their brief sojourn at Dumbarton Castle, she had been confined to the cargo well for so long that she still could smell the strange melding of tar, foodstuffs, and lamp oil. As soon as they stepped outside into the cool night air, Cora drew a deep breath that made Gavin smile again, causing her heart to flutter.

Ah, God, mayhap a walk wasn't so wise an idea after all...

"Come."

As if he had seen her turn slightly back to the door, he held her hand more firmly and drew her with him toward the center of the bailey, where the torchlight wasn't as bright as that shining from the ramparts. Cora felt near breathless when they finally stopped, his strides so much longer than hers that she had taken two steps for each one of Gavin's.

"There, now. Look up."

She did, gasping in awe at the midnight-blue sky strewn with glittering stars as far in each direction as she could see.

Yet a dark thought suddenly struck her. The last time she recalled lingering anywhere to survey the heavens had been the night she heard from her clansmen that Gavin was dead. Grief-stricken, she had contemplated throwing herself from the fortress tower... the pain too much to bear—

"Och, woman, I brought you out here tae delight you—not tae make you sad. Tell me what's plaguing you."

Gavin spoke so earnestly that Cora could not but look up at him, though she shook her head. "It's in the past... another lifetime and one thankfully behind me—"

"No, I would hear it. Anything that distresses you is of great distress tae me. Your voice is shaking, Cora..."

Aye, she trembled from head to foot to recall such heartache, such a terrible sense of loss. Gavin stepped closer to her, his hand clasping hers to his chest though he did not reach out to embrace her. She could feel his heartbeat through her fingers, so strong, so steady, though it seemed to speed up when she met his gaze, her eyes welling.

"A week after I married Seoras, word came from my clansmen that you had died. They lied tae me, I dinna know why. I stood atop a tower on a night much like this one. . . not wanting tae live. Yet I did go on. . . all this time believing you were dead, until the moment you hauled me from that wagon—"

"*Bastards.*"

Gavin clutched her hand so tightly now that it hurt, but she didn't try to pull away from him. In the torchlight, she could swear she saw moisture glistening in his eyes, too, though his jaw was clenched as if in fury.

Yet a moment later, a ragged sigh tore from him, and now he did draw her into his arms.

Not to try and kiss her, Cora stiffening at once, but to hold her tenderly as if trying to soothe her.

"You've suffered so much. . . for me. *For me,* Cora!"

The pain in his voice palpable, raw, she felt her throat tighten and her arms crept around him to try and comfort him, too.

"You agreed tae a devil's bargain tae save my life. . . protecting me, just as you seek tae protect me now from your clan. I know about King Robert's decrees—both of them. The messenger who accompanied us here, Ivor, told me all."

Her heart thundering, Cora went still in Gavin's arms, even as she realized she held onto him fiercely like she would never let him go.

He knew all! She found it suddenly difficult to breathe, the terrible weight she had carried since seeing Gavin again, threatening to choke her. . . until she felt the burden slip from her like the tears tumbling down her face.

Her body went limp against him, though she had no fear of falling for how fiercely he held her, too.

His arms tight around her. Her damp cheek pressed against his chest.

His heart beating hard and fast against her ear as they simply stood there together, beneath the stars.

"Cora, you know I love you... I've never stopped loving you. I believe you love me, too, but you dinna have tae say a word. I will wait for you as long as it takes... and one day I *will* hear you say that you want tae be my bride. We will be happy together for as long as God gives us... with a home and bairns—and you'll not think again of the past, for it will have all washed away. Do you hear me, lass?"

Aye, she heard him, Cora nodding against his chest. She had no voice with which to speak, such emotion overwhelmed her.

She had never felt more loved and cherished than in that moment, yet uncertainty still faced them.

A few days more... that's all she had to wait to know if they would be free to love each other or wrenched apart—dear God, please may it not be the latter.

"Come, let's return tae the great hall."

Again, Cora nodded, feeling bereft as he released her, though he reached for her hand and laced his fingers with hers.

With his other hand, he reached up and traced his thumb tenderly across her cheek to wipe away the dampness... first one and then the other, a smile tugging at his lips.

"All will be well, my love, I swear it—och, but we canna have those little girls thinking you've been crying. They're longing tae meet you. Will you summon a smile for them?"

"Aye, Gavin," she murmured, the pleased look on his handsome face making her wonder if he might take her again into his arms.

Mayhap even kiss her?

For the first time since they had been reunited, she yearned for him to press his lips to hers, astonishing herself and filling her with hope—but he only gave a low laugh and drew her with him toward the keep.

Cora blushed deeply to see that the guards stationed around the bailey had resumed their duties, clearly having stopped to watch her and Gavin standing together under the stars.

The wondrous, shimmering stars...

15

"Have your sword skills gone tae hell, man, or are you just distracted?"

Gavin sucked in a deep breath as his strapping, russet-haired cousin, Finlay, lowered his weapon to stare at him while wiping sweat from his own brow.

The air around them rang with swords striking swords, the bailey filled with men grunting and parrying while the midday sun beat down upon them.

Gabriel stood off to one side, watching the training with several other of his captains, Finlay having been given the task of crossing weapons with Gavin—och, it was true. He was distracted, his mind filled with thoughts of Cora.

The way she had looked last night in the torchlit bailey, the cool breeze lifting strands of her midnight hair, and her blue gown fitting her slender form to perfection.

The way she had felt in his arms as elation had filled him just to hold her.

The way she had looked into his eyes when he had wiped away her tears... aye, with love, he was certain of it, as deep and fervent as what he felt for her... his beloved Cora.

He had almost drawn her closer to kiss her for how expectantly her gaze had drifted to his mouth, her breath stilled... but he had forced himself to walk with her instead to the keep.

The right moment would come, aye, he just had to be patient, hope flooding him again that she would have even looked at him with yearning.

A good sign. A wonderful sign! With an exuberant roar, he raised his sword and swung at Finlay, who bellowed out a great laugh when steel struck steel, their blades ringing.

"Aye, that's better, cousin!" shouted the bearded warrior while Gavin laughed back at him, both of them circling each other only to strike—and then strike again.

The two of them so well-matched in strength and skill that neither had the better of the other, until Gabriel's command echoed around the bailey for everyone to lower their weapons.

"Not bad... for a raider," Finlay heaved out as he caught his breath, Gavin driving his sword into the dirt and leaning one arm upon the hilt.

"Not bad... for a landsman." His lungs burning, he grinned at Finlay as that same sense of camaraderie settled over him, aye, something he had missed for a very long time.

The world looked brighter to him today. The sun more brilliant, the sky bluer.

The future beckoned to him with such promise that Gavin couldn't help but feel enlivened. He thrust his fingers through his sweat-damp hair and glanced up at the tower that housed Cora, wondering if she had watched him.

As soon as they had returned to the great hall last night, Keira and Rhona had run laughing and squealing toward them and that had been the end of any further time alone for the evening.

He and Cora had sat near each other at the table, but always with the girls excitedly chattering between them... until Magdalene had called a gentle stop to it all an hour later and escorted them from the hall—Cora accompanying them.

Aye, she had left him staring after her while Gabriel had thrown him a wry smile and thrust a cup filled with ale into his hand.

"A lovesick laird if ever I've seen one. She needs her sleep, man—and we've got training in the morning. I'm curious tae see how well you raiders fight."

So Gavin hoped he had shown his cousin—at least near the end—as he drew another deep breath and pulled his sword out of the dirt to sheathe it in his belt.

As if reading his mind, Gabriel waved him over... though if Gavin had expected an appraisal of his skill with weapons, instead he found himself gaping in surprise and echoing what Gabriel had just told him.

"I'm invited tae luncheon in the garden?"

"Aye." Gabriel smiled at him as wryly as the night before. "Maggie and the girls love it there and want tae show the garden tae Cora—and you. Unless you've something more pressing tae do?"

Gavin shook his head even as Gabriel grimaced at him.

"Take care tae clean yourself up first, aye, a good dunking. For all the moon-eyed gazing you did at that tower, I'm amazing you worked up a sweat at all, but you're ripe. Go on with you."

Grinning, Gavin obliged him, his heart thundering as he sprinted across the bailey to an opposite tower where he had been quartered.

A last glance at Cora's window before he ducked inside made him all the more determined to hurry when he saw her standing there, watching him, though at once she disappeared into the room.

∽

AH, God, Cora felt breathless!

Yet it wasn't because Keira and Rhona, dressed in matching blue tunics, hastened her toward the garden by pulling her along, Magdalene hurrying behind them with a basket slung over her arm.

Cora felt as if her cheeks still burned from watching Gavin from her window. She had never stood fully in front, but off to one side so he wouldn't see her.

Her heart racing to look down upon him—just as her heart raced now.

Was it only last night since she had bid him goodnight in the great hall? So reluctantly, too, she couldn't deny it, though Magdalene had gently insisted that she needed to rest.

Rest? She had taken hours to fall asleep as she had relived over and over those astonishing moments under the stars.

Gavin had drawn from her something she had not thought to reveal to him until her remembered heartache had overwhelmed her.

Her pain becoming his pain as he had sought to comfort her while her heart had gone out to him—och, she could no longer withhold her love from him or even attempt to, no matter what news came from King Robert's messenger.

She had tossed and turned. . . feeling his arms around her.

The strength of him and yet his tenderness, too. His kindness and caring. . . his overwhelming concern for what *she* had suffered, though Gavin had suffered, too.

She had heard the anguish in his voice, the memory of it as she had lain awake staring at the canopy, filling her with shame.

Shame for spurning him over and again, though she had believed it was the only thing she could do to protect him. Yet all the while he had professed his love for her—dear God, for that alone she must ask for his forgiveness.

Even last night when she had thought to flee back to her room and then moments later, run back into the keep, Gavin had held onto her hand to draw her into the bailey. To think of what she would have missed if she had surrendered to her panic and left him standing there alone!

Gavin loved her. He wanted them to have a home together and children, Cora daring to hope after she had yearned to kiss him that mayhap she wasn't ruined after all and they could find happiness together—

"Lady Cora, look, we're here!"

Jarred from her rushing thoughts by little Rhona's unbridled excitement, Cora could not help but smile as Keira threw open the oaken door to the walled garden.

A shaky smile to be sure as she glanced over her shoulder for any sign of Gavin, but she didn't see him.

"Give him some time, Cora," came Magdalene's soft admonishment beside her, followed by a laugh. "He was training only moments ago."

Aye, she had watched him with her hand pressed to her breast, feeling her racing heartbeat as he thrust and parried with Finlay and dodged blow after lethal blow.

Her fearsome Highland raider. . . for Gavin *was* hers and she would never pretend it was otherwise ever again.

Like a revelation deep in the night after sleepless hours, Magdalene's words had flown back to her to fill her heart. . .

We canna protect them from harm no more than we can catch sunlight between our fingers. . . but we can love, Cora, with every breath, every kiss, every embrace.

Aye, so she would, from that moment on. . . though she prayed fervently it would be longer than a day, an hour.

The darkness of that thought stilling her breath, Cora nonetheless shook it off as best she could and followed the girls into the garden.

Rhona and Keira were fairly frolicking with joy to be in a place where they had spent much time with Magdalene, enjoying eating outdoors and tending to the roses.

Cora breathed deeply of the perfumed air, which enlivened her senses all the more. She could not resist glancing behind her to look through the open doorway, which made Magdalene laugh and take her by the hand.

"Come. We have a favorite spot over there by that tree stump."

Within a few moments, she and Magdalene were

seated upon a tartan blanket spread upon the ground, while the girls skipped and giggled along the sun-dappled paths.

Truly, the day was glorious and so rare a thing with summer waning and rainy days soon to outnumber fair ones.

The rich black dirt was still damp from morning dew, the earthen smell as heady a scent to Cora as the fragrant roses. Everything smelled wonderful. She leaned over to brush a streak of mud from her slipper as Magdalene began to spread the contents of her basket upon the blanket.

Fresh-baked oatcakes and wild raspberry jam sweetened with honey. A bowl of creamy white duck eggs boiled and peeled. A buttery apple tart that made Cora's mouth water as she pulled out the cork stopper from a narrow-mouthed pitcher and poured amber cider into five wooden cups. One for her, Magdalene, Keira, Rhona, and Gavin—

"You look happier, Cora."

She met Magdalene's gaze, her former sister-in-law one of the loveliest women she had ever seen and with as beautiful a spirit. Cora reached out to take her hand, gratitude overwhelming her.

"I am, thanks tae you. Your wise words have made all the difference."

"Och, it was only a matter of time before you realized yourself that you canna hold back love—but I hurried things along a wee bit. Here's Gavin now."

Cora must have gone stock-still at the sight of him entering the garden for Magdalene gave her hand a squeeze and then stood up, shaking out her gown.

"The girls and I will stay off in that far corner for a while and give you a chance tae greet each other. They love tae dig for worms."

"Worms?" Cora echoed, barely registering what Magdalene had just said as she watched Gavin stride toward them.

Tall and so powerfully built... his hair a burnished red in the sunlight.

His dark brown eyes riveted upon her just as hers were upon him, Cora scarcely realizing Magdalene had slipped away to leave them alone.

Ah, God, alone.

She felt her heartbeat pulsing in her throat as she hastened to rise and stepped off the blanket, one of her slippers catching upon an exposed root.

Gasping, she stumbled forward... straight into Gavin's arms. Yet instead of looking alarmed, he smiled at her so broadly that her heart skipped a beat. His expression was filled with good humor, so much like the first time she saw him two years ago when he offered her that wriggling herring...

"You did that on purpose, aye?"

His low teasing made her flush, Cora feeling thrilled and embarrassed by turns as she shook her head.

"My slipper... the root—"

"Och, and here I thought you were especially happy tae see me."

"I am happy tae see you!" Now Cora felt as if her cheeks were truly ablaze at how she'd blurted out at him, but Gavin only laughed.

A low, husky sound that made her feel as if she were melting inside, his arms still wrapped around her though he had righted her moments ago.

He gazed down at her and she gazed up at him, her hands pressed to his chest, her heart racing faster —until a shriek of delight from Rhona made them both turn around.

"Look at my worm! He's so big, aye?"

Magdalene and Keira's laughter mingled with Rhona's as Gavin chuckled, too, releasing Cora as he waved for them to come and join them.

"Bring that fine worm over here and I'll tell you a story. A big fish story!"

At once Keira and Rhona came running, with Magdalene hurrying after them, Cora grateful for a chance to catch her breath after how flustered she'd become.

Gavin sat down upon the stump while the rest of them settled upon the blanket, Magdalene handing everyone a cup of cider.

Cora watched in astonishment as Gavin drained his cup with one swallow and wiped his mouth with great exaggeration, tightly closing one eye and cackling as if he imitated some old fisherman.

"Hold up that wriggling worm, lass, and pretend you're threading it upon a hook—aye, that's it."

Rhona giggled as she obliged him, while Keira's eyes were round with fascination.

"Now cast your fishing line into the water—just as I did one gray, cloudy day off the coast of Argyll. The water so blue and deep I couldna see the bottom, nor could I see the worm once he sank down a good ways."

"Like this?" Sitting cross-legged, Rhona cast her imaginary line in the direction of a nearby apple tree, her eyes grown as wide as her sister's. Then she looked down as if peering over the side of a boat. "Oh, no, I canna see my worm!"

"Dinna worry, lass, he's still there, squirming away, and with all those hungry fish swimming around him. Do you know what happened next?"

Both girls shook their heads while Gavin chortled

as if with glee. "The most astonishing thing I've ever seen! I tugged upon that line a wee bit and suddenly, it went taut, aye, I knew I'd caught my supper. So I hauled it up, a fine brown sea trout, and was about to scoop it into my net when a bigger fish—twice the size and bright green—burst above the waves and swallowed my fish whole."

"Oh. . ." murmured Keira, entranced, while Rhona pretended to tug upon her line.

"Aye, I tugged hard, too, and was about tae haul that green fish into my boat when out of the deep came another fish, as big as a man and silvery blue, and swallowed my catch."

"Big as a man?" echoed Keira.

Gavin nodded and leaned closer while keeping his one eye scrunched closed. "I bent down tae drag that silver fish into my boat when out of the water leapt a giant fish as big as a whale—with its mouth wide open, and it swallowed that other fish whole! So you know what I did?"

Again, the girls shook their heads, though both looked doubtful now, as if they weren't quite sure any longer if they liked Gavin's story.

"Och, would *you* stay and wrestle with so mighty a beast?"

"No!" Rhona blurted quite decidedly.

"No. . ." murmured Keira, glancing from Magdalene to Cora, who whispered, "No," too.

"Aye, well, I didna have tae fight him! All of a sudden that giant creature gave a cough and out flew the silvery fish—and that one coughed and out came the green fish, and it coughed, too, and right into my boat flopped that brown sea trout. I had a fine supper after all. . . thanks tae one wee worm."

Rhona blinked as if absorbing it all and then burst out giggling, followed by Keira.

Magdalene glanced with relief at Cora, as if glad that Gavin's tale hadn't frightened them.

Both girls jumped up to give him a hug, and then Rhona scurried off toward the far corner of the garden.

"Rhona?" called out Magdalene.

"I want tae put my worm back in the hole so that giant fish canna find him!"

Everyone's laughter echoed around the garden as Keira ran to help her and then drew her sister back by the hand, the girls settling back down upon the blanket to enjoy their luncheon.

It didn't take long and their simple repast was nearly gone, Cora eating with more appetite than she'd felt for a long time as she found herself imagining Gavin telling such vivid tales to their bairns one day.

Mayhap he guessed her thoughts for his gaze rarely strayed from her, which made her face grow warm again and Magdalene to cast her a knowing look.

It seemed before Cora knew it, the remnants of their meal were packed in the basket, Magdalene urging Rhona and Keira to their feet.

Cora made to rise, too, but Magdalene waved her back down.

"No, no, stay and enjoy the garden."

Another few moments more and Cora and Gavin were alone... truly alone, the oaken door closing behind Magdalene and the girls.

Neither saying a word until he began to chuckle, shaking his head.

"I did see such a strange thing once... not long

after I apprenticed tae a fisherman. A fish as big as our boat swallowed three smaller ones—och, in truth, it chewed them tae bits with monstrous teeth, but I wasna going tae tell that tae the bairns. The sight frightened me so much, I told old William I would never return tae the sea."

16

Cora stared at Gavin in surprise; she couldn't imagine him being afraid of anything.

"What happened?" she queried softly, which made him chuckle again, though he sobered and shrugged.

"I needed a trade so I could provide for myself and my mother. I went back tae the sea."

Cora felt her breath catch as remorse flooded her.

Ah, God, she had spoken so cruelly to him a few days ago to say that he was nothing but a fisherman. She had said so many awful things to spurn him.

"Gavin... forgive me. I behaved so terribly towards you, but I didna mean a word of it—"

"Not a word, lass?"

He searched her eyes so intently... not in anger but as if he sought some reassurance, which made her feel even worse tae have scorned him so convincingly.

"No, no... it wasna true that I never wanted tae marry you. You were everything tae me—all I dreamed was one day becoming your wife. I thought my serving maid loyal tae me and shared my hopes with her, and she went tae Rory! He told me if I didna agree tae wed Seoras that they would kill you—God help me, what else was I tae do?"

Tears filled her eyes, but she did her best to blink them away as Gavin reached for her. Yet she shifted backward upon the blanket, determined to tell him all before he did anything to try and soothe her.

"That day was the worst one of my life—saying goodbye tae you in the church. It was true, I couldna marry you and had agreed tae marry another man, but only so my clansmen would spare your life! Yet it wasna over, even then. All I heard was that they had escorted you out of the stronghold—"

"*Escorted*," Gavin broke in bitterly, though Cora rushed on.

"Aye, so I thought, until you told me that my clansmen had gone tae the village the next morning looking for you, I'm certain tae slay you. Rory had sworn as much as I lay weeping upon the floor of the great hall. They vowed tae kill you if you ever came near me again, so they must have believed you would refuse tae flee Argyll. Yet you escaped from them, thank God, you escaped!"

Cora rose shakily to her feet and almost stumbled again, her slipper entangling in the blanket, but she righted herself before Gavin could reach her. She shook her head in disbelief as a sudden realization came to her.

"They lied tae me about your death tae kill any hope that somehow a miracle might bring us back together. I'm certain all this time they've kept looking for you—just as they're searching for you now. At least until King Robert's decrees sway them—*if* they sway them... oh, God!"

Now Cora did falter, the brilliant sunlight and her

favorite scent of roses mocking her as her knees gave way—only to have Gavin catch her.

He pulled her into his arms to hold her close, smoothing her hair, whispering her name and that he loved her. She buried her face into his chest and once again found comfort in the steady beating of his heart, though her new resolve to not withhold her love from him any longer was flagging.

"Maggie told me we canna protect the ones we love from harm no more than we can catch sunlight between our fingers—and it's true, Gavin! I was wrong to think if I had nothing more tae do with you ever again, you would be safe, but part of me still believes it. I couldna bear tae be the cause of your death—"

"No, we willna speak of death, only our life together." Gavin's arms had tightened around her, his voice grown hoarse. "You have protected me as much as anyone could by making a plea tae the king on my behalf. Rory and your clansmen willna dare tae defy him, so we must have faith that all will transpire as it was meant tae be. Can you do that for me as well, Cora?"

She nodded, blinking away tears again as she lifted her head to look at him... her beloved.

Gavin reached up to stroke her cheek so tenderly, she didn't have the heart to say to him that mayhap he accredited more honor to Rory than her ambitious cousin possessed.

Her clan's loyalty to Robert the Bruce was still largely untried, though they had proved themselves the night Gabriel, Cameron, and Conall saved the king's life—and freed Cora forever from the man she hated.

"No more dark thoughts," Gavin bade her as if reading her mind, his gaze falling to her lips.

The same yearning for him to kiss her overcame Cora, but she stiffened, too, mayhap simply by thinking of Seoras. At once she felt Gavin's arms relax around her, and he looked concerned as if he had somehow distressed her.

Dear God, how was she ever going to be free of the nightmare she'd known in her marriage if she didn't take a step... even if only a small one?

"Gavin... dinna let me go, please."

He looked startled, but it passed quickly as he drew her close again, his arms so strong and protective around her.

She knew Gavin would never hurt her, that certainty filling her with a longing even stronger than before as she lifted her face to him.

"Kiss me, Gavin. Help me tae forget..."

As if she had bestowed upon him the greatest gift, he stared at her in fresh surprise and wonder... and then bent his head to press his lips to hers.

So lightly and with such heart-stopping gentleness that her breath caught from the sweetness of it, tears of relief and joy filling Cora's eyes.

She hadn't thought for even an instant to pull away. She parted her lips and pressed them more fervently to Gavin's, only to hear a muted groan from him... and she would swear that she felt him trembling.

Or mayhap it was her as she lifted her hands to cradle his face, Cora swept by a dizzying sensation so like when she had kissed him during their secret meetings in the church.

Gavin, the love of her life.

"Cora..."

His murmur against her lips made her open her

eyes to see him raise his head to gaze at her, moisture glistening in his eyes.

This powerful raider, who had become one of King Robert's own warriors, filled with the deepest and truest of emotion... for her.

"I love you, lass... more than you'll ever know."

The same words flew to her lips, but before she could utter them, he lowered his head to kiss her again.

His mouth covering hers with more stirring pressure this time, though still so tender that her knees again felt weak.

The delicious shivers coursing through her stoking blazing hope that the torment of her marriage was behind her—no, she would not think of it any longer!

Not when Gavin was holding her as if he would never let her go... Cora's arms encircling his neck to draw him closer.

She felt the tip of his tongue parting her lips and she moaned softly, Gavin answering her with a hoarse sigh against her mouth as he crushed her against him.

His embrace grown impassioned and his deepening kiss making all else seem to disappear around them as she swirled her tongue with his in so intimate a way that she trembled from the wonder of it.

He was shaking, too, and she heard him groan as he eased his hold upon her, which made her cling to him all the more and brokenly whisper his name. Yet it wasn't her voice that made her start, but a man's urgent outcry that broke through the entrancing spell that gripped her.

"*Gavin!*"

His arms fell from around her so abruptly that she swayed, but he caught her by the forearms to steady her as they both turned to see Gabriel striding into the garden.

"Your ship, man! It's afire!"

A vehement curse escaped from Gavin and he drew her with him to meet Gabriel, whose expression was dark with fury.

"A ship sailed past like a phantom, the crew loosing flaming arrows onto the deck before my men could fire back in kind. They're fighting the blaze, but it's taken hold—"

"Ranulf MacDougall, it has tae be," cut in Gavin, his grip upon Cora's hand so tight that she winced. "We must launch the other two ships and give chase—"

"Aye, I already ordered all of your crewmen tae the loch. Let us go!"

Cora felt her heart thundering in her throat as Gavin pressed a kiss to her cheek.

"Find Maggie and stay close tae her."

He didn't say anything more, but left her and followed Gabriel from the garden, while Cora hastened after them.

By the time she had reached the doorway, the two men were running hard across the bailey toward where whinnying horses were being held for them by stable hands.

Another few moments and Gavin and Gabriel had ridden through the gates, accompanied by a host of grim-faced warriors as it seemed the entire castle had erupted in commotion.

"Cora!"

She heard Magdalene's voice and saw her outside the entrance to the keep, Cora feeling heartsick as she lifted the hem of her gown and ran, too.

Gavin would soon be aboard one of his new ships

and mayhap sailing into battle and she hadn't told him that she loved him—dear God, please may she still have the chance!

~

IN THE DIMMING TWILIGHT, Gavin stared grimly at the charred and smoking remains of what had been his raiding ship, Brody uttering a curse of dismay beside him.

Standing in the stern of one of the two new birlinns awarded to him by King Robert, Gavin could see Gabriel and his men assembled ashore to greet them —but the news he brought back with him wasn't what he had hoped.

Ranulf and his crew had enjoyed too far a lead for Gavin to catch up with them, and a stiff headwind hadn't helped their cause.

That bastard couldn't have executed a better surprise attack upon the beached ships, though it amazed Gavin still that only his birlinn had been the target of the raid as if Ranulf had purposely wanted to burn it alone.

At any other time, Gavin and his crew would have been out at sea and ably put out the flames as they had done on numerous occasions during their own raids—instead of on dry land and with his ship left with only a skeleton crew aboard. He blamed himself for that blunder, the arrows so thick during the attack that his four men had been unable to douse so many blazes, even with the help of the warriors Gabriel had posted on shore to guard the ships.

They were landsmen and with little skill at shoving vessels into the water quickly to thwart a raid, which had come on so swiftly, even his own crewmen were taken unawares by a ship that had appeared as if out of nowhere.

Ranulf had bested them, aye, most likely out of pure spite that he had been outrun the other day and that his quest to find those two chests of gold hidden at the island had proved fruitless.

"Och, at least the king's gold was saved," Brody said under his breath, guessing the direction of Gavin's thoughts.

He could thank his skeleton crew's quick thinking for emptying out a good part of the cargo well when it became clear they couldn't quell the flames on deck—the iron-banded chest hoisted onto the birlinn that Gavin stood upon now.

Between his own men and those that King Robert had given over to his command, he had more crewmen than he needed for the two ships that remained, at least until those other thirteen ships arrived. Both birlinns were crowded to the gills—another factor that had slowed them down—but he was proud of the men for the chase they had given Ranulf, albeit unsuccessful.

"Damn him," Gavin muttered, sickened to see what remained of his raiding ship, not enough left even to salvage.

Gabriel appeared disgusted, too, by the devastation as he and his men drew their horses nearer to the shoreline to greet the ships—though something else pricked Gavin's intuition at the way Gabriel looked at him as if he had more grim news to share.

Cora...

God help him, had something happened to her? He had bade her to find Magdalene, which meant she would have hurried back to the keep. The bailey had been so filled with commotion, neighing horses and men shouting—och, had there been an accident as she hastened to oblige him?

His heart pounding, Gavin didn't wait for the crewmen to jump overboard into the thigh-high water to bodily draw the birlinn up onto the pebbly beach. He lunged over the railing himself and landed with a splash of salt spray.

Gabriel at once steered his snorting stallion closer to meet him, which made Gavin's throat tighten all the more as he strode to shore.

"Dinna tell me something is amiss with Cora."

"She's well, cousin, but sorely distressed. Rory Campbell and his clansmen arrived while you were gone and you willna be pleased by what he has tae say."

17

Cora stood stiff with tension beside Magdalene, the torchlit great hall in a tumultuous uproar.

On one side was Rory Campbell flanked by three of his senior clansmen, his scowl in her direction unrelenting since she had entered with Magdalene a short while ago at the behest of Gabriel.

As the earl of MacLachlan Castle, he stood at the center of the hall while to his right were his own clansmen, many of them brandishing their fists at Rory and hurling curses.

The midnight-haired chieftain—a formidable-looking man though he was neither as tall nor broad-shouldered as Cameron and Conall, cousins he shared with Cora—ignored the taunts and narrowed his gaze at Gavin, who stood next to Gabriel.

Cora felt an icy chill as Rory's expression grew thunderous, though Magdalene squeezed her hand to offer reassurance.

"It seems, *Baron* MacLachlan, that you have won the favor of King Robert, along with his protection. I've been made known of your astounding good fortune by not only the two royal messengers sent tae me from Dumbarton Castle—but by that one there, Ivor, who accompanied you on your ship. The king clearly didna wish for any lack of understanding that his decree has freed you from our vow tae seek your death if you have aught tae do with Cora Campbell."

"So you agree tae it, man?" Gabriel interjected with sternness, Cora feeling weak inside as Rory gave him a brusque nod.

"Say it loud for everyone tae hear," came Gavin's equally forceful demand, to which the chieftain bristled.

"*Aye*, I agree tae it."

Swamping relief swept Cora as a great roar went up from the assembled clansmen, though Rory and his men still appeared stiff-shouldered and grim-faced.

Within moments of her entering the hall earlier, her cousin had grudgingly proclaimed her free of her clan to conduct her life however she chose—both of King Robert's decrees now accepted and agreed to, thank God. She should feel joyous, elated, but something was amiss, Cora could sense it.

It had been Magdalene who had run to her bedchamber to tell her that the chieftain and his clansmen had arrived outside the castle gates, and with Gavin still gone after Ranulf.

Apprehension had at once flooded Cora, though Magdalene had done her best to calm her as Gabriel had rode out to speak to Rory. Yet he hadn't looked pleased when he returned, though he revealed nothing to either his wife or Cora.

No more than an hour later, word had come that Gavin's ships were returning, which had sent Gabriel riding out again to meet him. Rory and his men had been ordered to wait further from the castle while

Gavin returned alongside Gabriel, and only then was the chieftain allowed to enter the gates with his three clansmen as the rest of them were guarded closely by Gabriel's warriors.

Now here they all stood at what should have been a moment to celebrate... yet something still didn't feel right—Cora looking with confusion at Magdalene. Her former sister-in-law appeared confused as well as they glanced back at Gabriel and Gavin, both men far too somber.

"Speak what else has brought you here today, Rory, and let's have this thing out!" Gabriel commanded, his voice strained with fury. "You said it's a trial by combat that you're after?"

Trial by combat? A terrible intuition gripping her as Rory nodded with as much barely restrained anger, Cora felt Magdalene again squeeze her hand though she felt as if her fingers had gone numb.

"Aye, between Gavin MacLachlan and a kinsman of the man he murdered five days past at my stronghold—"

"*It was no murder!*"

Gavin's disavowal ringing from the rafters, the entire assemblage fell silent while Cora's heartbeat seemed to thunder in her ears.

"I came upon the man while making my escape and he challenged me, drawing his sword. The fight was a fair one and he fell tae my blade."

"Aye, grievously wounded, *after* you had trespassed upon our land and cut him down," countered Rory, his face grown red. "He died hours later—an agonizing death that we deem a murder most foul. Will you take a coward's path, MacLachlan? Or will you accept Blair Campbell's right tae trial by combat on behalf of his brother, and allow *God* tae decide who is right and who is wrong?"

Cora held her breath as Gavin appeared startled by the name of his opponent, though it was fleeting as he stepped forward, his expression set as if in stone.

"I accept your challenge."

No roar greeted Gavin's harshly spoken words, only a low rumble as clansmen spoke in astonishment among themselves until Gabriel waved his hand for silence.

"At dawn, then, the two shall meet at the center of the bailey—"

"No, *now!*" demanded Rory as the great hall erupted again in jeers directed at the chieftain. "A night's sleep willna make any difference tae the outcome. My warrior will prevail either way, so let's see this thing done!"

"Listen tae me, Gavin, you dinna have tae do this tonight. . ." Cora heard Gabriel say in a fierce aside, her heart sinking at the hard set of Gavin's jaw. She saw him glance in her direction, his eyes as inscrutable as his face, and then he nodded at Rory.

"Very well. Now."

Cora clapped her hands over her ears at the deafening clamor as Rory and his three clansmen strode first from the great hall, followed by Gabriel and Gavin and all those in attendance who surged outside —except for herself and Magdalene.

Her former sister-in-law had laced her arm around Cora's waist as if to hold her back, but there was no need. Cora stood rooted to the floor.

Stunned. Sickened. Horrified by the swift turn of events from what should have been the most wondrous moment, her and Gavin at last having the chance to be together—to one of abject fear.

"No, you mustna think harm will befall him!" insisted Magdalene as Cora somehow moved one foot in front of the other to sink onto a nearby bench. "Have courage, Cora. Have faith. Ah, God, we must pray."

"SO WE MEET AGAIN, *TROUT*."

Disdain burned in Blair Campbell's dark eyes as Gavin stared at the strongly muscled man he had once considered a friend—but who had been no friend to him at all.

A man he had served with as a guard at Rory's stronghold atop the palisades and then within the chieftain's own hall.

All so Gavin could be close to Cora... always Cora.

The stricken look she had thrown him as he left the hall, surrounded by his shouting clansmen, made him yearn for her even now, his throat tightening—och, God, he could not allow himself to think of her, not if he wanted to live!

Standing in the center of the bailey, Gavin had awaited Blair's arrival with one hand clutching his sword and the other, a thick wooden shield.

His opponent had been left with the rest of Rory's clansmen outside the castle, but it hadn't taken Blair long to ride into the bailey atop a powerful steed as if he had known all along he would be summoned.

Aye, Gavin had taken the bait, but why not see this thing done? A full year of hatred for Rory and his clansmen welled up inside of him, his hand having become a fist upon the sword hilt and his jaw clenched as tightly.

"I should have killed you the day we threw you out, MacLachlan," taunted Blair as he dismounted and turned to face Gavin with his own sword and shield in hand. "Anything tae spare my brother the fate you dealt him. *Murderer!*"

Gavin didn't respond, for there was no point any longer in trying to change any Campbell's mind. The entire matter would soon be decided in blood, and he slowly began to circle his opponent.

"Aye, your silence bespeaks your guilt, man," grated Blair, circling now, too, as the bailey grew quiet but for shuffling of their feet in the dirt and the nervous whinnying of horses.

Out of the corner of his eye, Gavin saw Gabriel intently watching the two of them, and Rory as well, but then he focused again on the only man that mattered right now... the one that wanted to kill him.

Somehow he quelled any exhaustion from the long day, just as he'd done out on the sea when no sleep would be afforded until they had sailed far away from the scene of a raid. Breathing slowly and deeply, Gavin could feel every muscle, every bone alive with tension for the battle to come—

"By God, MacLachlan, you will pay!"

Gavin dodged Blair's vicious sword blow in the nick of time and almost tripped, which made the onlookers encircled around them gasp and draw even closer, locking arms.

There would be no escape for either of them, but Gavin had no intention of retreating. He made as if to glance away for an instant and then brought his sword down upon Blair's with such force that metal rang against metal.

"Aye, Trout, trick me off my guard. No less than I'd expect from a man who wooed the chieftain's cousin in secret as if you ever had any chance with her—"

"She will be my *wife*, man, this very night if she'll

have me and as soon as I'm finished with you." Gavin circled again and brandished his sword, the blade flashing brightly in the torchlight.

The glint caught Blair in the eye, which made him curse and throw all of his weight behind a blow so filled with force and fury that Gavin's shield was knocked from his hand.

Again the onlookers gasped, some cursing, too. A clansman rushed forward with another shield for Gavin, though he waved it away. The thing was proving too ponderous, and he circled faster now while Blair sneered at him.

"My thanks for making my task easier, fool!"

With a roar, Blair lunged with such driving momentum that Gavin was knocked onto one knee as he blocked the blow—but he was up within an instant and swung his sword around to ring against his opponent's upraised weapon.

It happened so fast, the blade sliding down to cut into Blair's upper right arm. He screamed in pain, dropping his shield and backing away from Gavin as if he couldn't believe he had been struck.

"Enough, the matter is settled!" commanded Gabriel, but Blair appeared not to hear him as he rushed wildly at Gavin with a thrust meant to disembowel him.

One sidestep and Gavin shifted cleanly out of the way. Blair went spilling headlong into the dirt, roaring in disbelief as his sword flew from his hand.

Gavin was upon him even as the man rolled over, still howling in fury.

The bloodied tip of his sword pressed in so deadly a manner to Blair's throat that he could but lie still with his limbs askew and his breathing ragged.

Gavin steadied his own breath through clenched

teeth. "Enough, man. The thing is done as Earl Gabriel said. I didna murder your brother and I *willna* slay you. Now stand up."

The onlookers stared in amazement as Gavin drew back his sword and offered his hand to Blair, who looked up at Gavin as if he couldn't believe he had been offered mercy.

"Get up, Blair, your wound needs tending. You'll not honor your brother by dying, but by living."

With a pained grimace, Blair clasped Gavin's hand and was pulled to his feet. Rory came forward to throw his arm around his clansman's shoulders to help support him while Gabriel gave an order to several of his men to take the injured man to the infirmary.

As Blair was escorted away, the chieftain stared at Gavin as if he couldn't believe, either, that his clansman had been spared, and he seemed about to say something when a feminine outcry pierced the air.

"*Gavin!*"

He stepped back as Cora pushed her way through the onlookers to rush toward him, tears shimmering in her eyes.

She stopped cold just shy of him, her widened gaze sweeping him from head to foot as if she couldn't believe he was unharmed, and then turned to Rory.

"Will you stop this madness now, cousin? I love Gavin and I *will* marry him. Pray give us some peace at last—"

"You love me, lass?"

Cora met Gavin's eyes, and she trembled as much as her voice had shaken with emotion to address Rory. "Aye, with all my heart."

"Then it's a wedding we'll be needing," Rory interjected, reaching out to grasp Gavin's hand. "You surprised me this day, Baron MacLachlan, and I willna forget it. You havna asked me and I doubt that you would, but you and Cora have the blessing of Clan Campbell."

Gavin felt astonished himself at the chieftain's powerful handclasp while the bailey erupted in thunderous roars of approval, even Gabriel looking amazed by what had just transpired.

Yet the one that looked overcome with joy was Cora. She hadn't moved an inch, her gaze upon Gavin alone as he sheathed his sword and closed the short distance between them to draw her into his arms.

His beloved—aye, she loved him! Wanted to marry him. He longed to kiss her, but blood had been shed upon this spot and he didn't know if she would welcome—

"Gavin, kiss me."

He did, pressing his lips fervently to hers as great shouts echoed around the bailey, though another feminine voice rose above the melee.

"If there's tae be a wedding, then I'll be making preparations with the bride!"

Gavin lifted his head to see Magdalene moving with great determination through the throng that had parted for her, Gabriel taking her hand and accompanying her the last few steps.

"I believe Gavin said he would wed her this very night, wife—if Cora will have him."

"Aye, well, I think we both can see that she'll have him, husband. Her prayers have been answered more richly than any of us could have imagined—but there will be no hasty ceremony tonight. With the Campbells in accordance and this unfortunate strife behind us, we're going tae have a proper wedding for the two of them, aye, and there's much for us tae do. Three days from now should be enough time tae make all the preparations and invite the guests—"

"Three days?" Gavin echoed, keen disappointment ripping through him as Magdalene looped her arm through Cora's and drew her away. "Guests?"

"For shame, Baron. Will you not have us bestow upon your beautiful bride the ceremony and wedding feast she deserves?"

Gavin could see humor flashing in Magdalene's green eyes, though Cora looked at him longingly. So much so that he was tempted to reclaim her and insist that they wed that very night, until Gabriel clapped him on the back.

"Dinna try tae dissuade her, man, I learned that well enough about Maggie. Three days will pass quickly, aye, I promise tae keep you busy—"

"So you must, husband, for these two willna see each other again until it's their wedding day!"

That pronouncement from Magdalene made Gavin groan in disbelief, but already she was leading Cora toward the keep.

Another clap on the back came from Gabriel, who smiled wryly at him.

"You need a good draught of ale, cousin—and Rory, you and your men are welcome tae stay for the wedding. Will you join us for a cup in the great hall?"

"Aye!"

Chapter 19

Cora stood in the middle of her bedchamber as Magdalene and her maidservants made last adjustments to her gown and the imported French lace fashioned into a veil.

Her wedding day. Happiness overflowed within

her and feminine laughter surrounded her, the early afternoon sun spilling through the window lighting a scene that thrilled her heart.

Her mother, Glenis, sat upon a chair and beamed at the proceedings, along with Aislinn, her cousin Cameron's beautiful red-haired wife, and Lisette, her cousin Conall's sweet-natured bride of little more than a month.

The two young women felt like the dearest of sisters to Cora now, their arrival with their strapping midnight-haired husbands yesterday, along with her parents from north Argyll, another amazing feat accomplished by Gabriel and Magdalene.

They had sent out messengers the very night Cora had professed her love to Gavin, to bid their special guests to attend the wedding festivities, though it had been Rory Campbell himself who rode back to his stronghold to escort an elated Owen and Glenis to MacLachlan Castle.

Cora had been told all of this by Magdalene, since for the past three days she had remained in her bedchamber—except for a quick visit to view the chapel—while preparations had reached a fever pitch downstairs.

Her desire to see Gavin again had swelled, too, and now Cora felt like she might burst from longing for him.

She had only glimpsed him three or so times from the window when he had stood in the bailey to look up at her—but it hadn't taken long for Gabriel or one of her cousins to slap him on the back and hustle him along, their good-natured ribbing carrying to her.

Their laughter, too. It seemed the entire castle was filled with high spirits that echoed up the tower steps and made her all the more eager for her wedding day to arrive.

Now it was finally here, little Rhona clapping her hands together as she and Keira stared with awe at Cora.

"You look like a princess," breathed Rhona as Keira reached out to touch the shimmering silver satin of Cora's gown.

"It's so pretty. Mama, will I wear a dress like this one day?"

"Aye, love," Magdalene assured her, Cora still astounded at the richness of the fabric imported as well from France.

Magdalene had set a host of village seamstresses to work over the past few days to create a half dozen new gowns for her in an array of colors, just as she had done for Aislinn. Gabriel's late brother, Malcolm, had bought an extravagant amount of fabrics for his wife, and Magdalene was determined to put the stuff to good use for all those she considered her family:

Cameron and Aislinn and their adopted daughter, Sorcha, who stood alongside Keira and stared at Cora, too, the thirteen-year-old girl truly lovely to behold in her blue silk gown. Cora had never seen such light blond hair, aye, the color of sunlight, contrasting with the bluest eyes, as bright as her smile.

Conall and Lisette, who had the most gentle expression and the softest brown eyes, and Conall's rambunctious four-year-old son, Colin. The little boy had been the only male allowed in Cora's room, his exuberant energy making her laugh and wish all the more for bairns of her own... especially when she learned from Magdalene and Aislinn that they were both expecting babies. Such wondrous news!

And now Cora and Gavin... *Cora and Gavin.* Just

thinking of their two names together made such joy brim inside Cora that tears blurred her eyes, but she blinked them away.

"Och, daughter, happy tears are always welcome." Glenis had risen from her chair and come over to embrace her, tears shining in her eyes, too. "When Gavin rushed into our home looking for you, he swore tae take care of you and I knew he would honor his vow. I never stopped praying that he would find you—and he did! God's blessings on you, my dearest Cora."

Her mother's tender kiss upon her cheek the sweetest gift, Cora bent down so Keira and Rhona could kiss her—followed by Sorcha, Aislinn, Lisette, and then Magdalene... so many kisses and hugs and joyous tears all around.

Until a sudden rap upon the door made them whirl around in a swish of silk and satin, a maidservant popping her head into the room.

"Earl Gabriel sent me tae tell you they're waiting in the chapel—"

"Och, men... always so impatient," Magdalene said with feigned annoyance, smiling at Cora. "I imagine your Gavin canna wait tae see you after three long days, aye?"

"My Gavin..." she murmured, for truly he was hers, and she couldn't wait to see him, either.

Trembling with anticipation, Cora felt as if she were floating as she accompanied Magdalene from the room, with everyone else following behind—a sweet cacophony of giggling and excited feminine voices.

Thankfully they had only to descend one flight of tower steps to the second floor, the heavy oak door of the chapel yawning open for them.

Cora already knew the space was small—the room consisting of a white-clothed altar and two carved benches on both sides of the narrow aisle—and she wondered as they drew closer how they would all fit inside.

Yet all thought seemed to flee as she spied Gavin standing so tall and handsome next to the altar, his dark brown eyes intense upon her as Magdalene led her into the room.

Her heart beating faster, her breath catching in her throat at how truly magnificent he looked in a deep blue tunic, and a plaid breacan draped over one broad shoulder and wound around his waist.

It seemed she had no more than blinked and she stood next to him, the two of them pressed close together as everyone squeezed in beside and behind them, the chapel completely full.

"Baron MacLachlan... Lady Cora," began the young priest, Father Timothy, whom she had met during her brief visit the other day. "Please join hands."

She gasped softly at the warmth of Gavin's fingers lacing with hers and then the sacred ceremony began. . . a spellbinding mix of his deep, beloved voice saying vows followed by hers, the scent of candles burning and the sweet smell of incense, and the rustling movements, childish whispers, and murmured prayers of those watching.

All she knew when the service was done was that Gavin clasped her hand more tightly and brought her fingers to his lips to kiss them.

Everything she had so longed for, dreamed of, and prayed for culminating in the tender pressure of his mouth against her skin, the stirring warmth of his breath the sweetest pronouncement of their union as husband and wife.

A resounding roar of congratulations went up

from the men—Cameron, Conall, Gabriel, her father, and even Brody and Rory Campbell amidst the crush of onlookers—while the women laughed and urged their menfolk to leave the chapel so the newly married couple might have a moment alone, the young ones already skittering out the door.

Another few moments and the chapel was empty but for Cora and Gavin, Father Timothy extinguishing the candles and then quickly exiting, too.

All the while, Gavin hadn't taken his eyes from her face, his hand still clasping hers, which he now held against his heart.

"My wife... at last."

His voice husky with emotion, Cora nodded, murmuring, "My husband... at last."

Only then did Gavin lower his head to kiss her and she leaned into him, melting against his chest as his lips moved over hers so gently at first.

Then so fervently, as if sealing their union again just for the two of them.

She felt lightheaded when he lifted his head to stare down at her, holding her close.

So close she could feel his heartbeat against her breast, and she knew that he must feel her heart beating, too.

"My beautiful bride... Cora."

His words sounding like a prayer of gratitude, she had once thought such joy would never be hers... but she cast the thought away, no darkness allowed this day. She stood on tiptoes to press her own kiss to his lips... only to hear a soft giggle at the doorway.

Somehow little Rhona had been left behind as everyone had headed downstairs to the great hall, but she didn't appear upset at all... instead smiling from ear to ear as she ran to them and hugged Cora around the knees.

"So pretty..."

"Aye, child, she is, indeed." Gavin cast so admiring a smile at Cora that she felt a blush burn her cheeks. He released her with a laugh as stirring to her heart, and swung Rhona up into his arms.

"Shall we join the others for a wedding feast?"

Rhona bobbed her curly head, giggling. Gavin reached for Cora's hand and together they left the chapel, the sweet smell of incense drifting after them.

"Look, Gavin! King Robert is here for our wedding feast."

Gavin followed Cora's astonished gaze to the wildflower-festooned dais where their empty seats awaited them, the king sitting between Gabriel and Magdalene.

"He said his men would be marching north, aye, he's paying us a fine tribute," Gavin murmured, squeezing Cora's hand.

His *wife's* hand... the wonder of it still sinking in with him as the assembled guests roared out a greeting that seemed to shake the rafters.

If he had thought that small chapel crowded, the great hall couldn't have held any more people, every bench, every table, every corner filled with well-wishers.

All of them waving and cheering for him and Cora as they walked together toward the dais, where everyone who had attended their wedding was seated, too. Her hand trembled now, which made Gavin draw her closer and wind an arm protectively around her waist.

Not because he was concerned anyone would do something untoward, but simply because he wanted her to feel him near her and to show he cared how she was feeling...always.

She glanced at him and smiled, a tremulous smile that Gavin imagined was more due to their rousing welcome, the clamor deafening.

Yet as soon as they reached the dais, Gabriel stood to walk over and meet them, everyone falling silent as if waiting expectantly.

Little sound but for the creaking of benches as clansmen, their wives, and children craned their necks for a better view while Gavin gave Cora over to Gabriel, who gallantly escorted her to her chair.

Even that short amount of time away from her side was too much for him and he strode to take his place beside her as Gabriel raised his voice to the throng.

"May I present Baron MacLachlan and his lovely bride, Cora MacLachlan!"

That resounding pronouncement elicited such a thunderous cheer and the stamping of feet that Gavin doubted he had ever heard such enthusiastic acclamation.

For him and Cora. Everyone truly appearing delighted for them—ah, God, if they only knew the trials they had both endured to arrive at this incredible moment.

Gavin didn't wait for Gabriel as host to pull out Cora's chair, but did so himself, which made his cousin shake his head and laugh.

"Aye, man, you're the eager bridegroom if ever I've seen one."

That wry comment made everyone in earshot

laugh, too, including Robert the Bruce, who pushed away from his chair to stand and lift his brimming cup in a toast.

At once the entire hall again fell silent, Gavin awed by the respect shown the King of Scots, from young and old alike.

"I sent the baron and his lady tae MacLachlan Castle hoping for this outcome, and though my decrees elicited high emotion in all involved and a wee bit of swordplay"—the king cast a glance at Rory Campbell, who gave him a rueful smile—"it's clear that all is as it should be. A marriage between the newly appointed commander of my western fleet and a most courageous and deserving young woman tae whom, along with others present in this hall, I owe my life. My deepest congratulations tae you both!"

Cups could be heard clinking together throughout the hall as everyone toasted them, Gavin leaning down to press a kiss to Cora's flushed cheek.

Her beautiful eyes brimmed with emotion at the great kindness displayed toward them, which made him take his seat beside her and clasp her hand.

He had never seen her look more stunning than in her silvery gown, the delicate veil covering her long, midnight hair like a crown of gossamer. Yet she appeared touchingly vulnerable, too, and he could well imagine what she must be thinking.

After the wedding feast came their wedding night. God help him, he would never do anything to rush her or alarm her, Gavin ready to take all the time she might need before they would even consummate their marriage.

He would be grateful just to hold her in his arms and feel her sleeping against him—her sudden intake of breath making him wonder if she had read his thoughts.

"Cora?"

She had turned to look into his eyes, those great blue pools reflecting a depth of feeling that so matched his own. She whispered his name, her words clearly meant for his ears alone.

"I know you will never hurt me. I love you..."

Staring at her with his heart pounding, Gavin barely heard Gabriel utter the command for the feast to begin.

Even when the kitchen doors at one end of the hall burst open and servants spilled forth with platters held high, he did not tear his gaze from her as he leaned forward to whisper in her ear, "And I you, my beloved. Always."

18

Cora watched wide-eyed, her heartbeat drumming in her ears, as Gavin shut the door with great force against the clansmen who had boisterously followed them to their bedchamber.

It was a miracle they hadn't shoved their way into the candlelit room, but his formidable strength and size had blocked them all—the iron bolt sliding into place with a resounding thud.

He stood there for a long moment, leaning upon the door and shaking his head as drunken shouts and good wishes, aye, some ribald remarks, too, faded down the hallway.

The wild melee had begun the moment Gavin had taken Cora by the hand and helped her to rise from the table. The two of them nearly surrounded as soon as they stepped foot from the dais, and there hadn't been anything Gabriel or King Robert or anyone else could have done, it all happened so fast.

Cora leaned against the foot of the bed, still stunned by how Gavin had lifted her into his arms and sprinted with her from the hall and up the tower steps, with the unruly hoard on their heels—ah, God, she couldn't help it as she began to giggle.

Gavin chuckled, too, still shaking his head as he slowly turned around as if he couldn't believe, either, the spectacle they must have made.

He looked disheveled, his queue undone and his hair loose, his breacan askew from all the pushing and struggling to shut the door, which only made Cora's giggles louder.

She pressed her hand to her mouth, but she couldn't contain her mirth, doubling over and laughing harder as Gavin's full-throated laughter joined with hers.

She would never have imagined their wedding night would begin in so merry a manner, but it felt good to laugh. She could not remember when she had last done so, and she wondered if Gavin was thinking the same thing.

His laughter was fading into chuckling, just as hers had quieted to an occasional giggle. She straightened to look at him, smiling and shaking her head.

"Your clansmen are a rowdy lot, husband."

He didn't answer, sobering altogether and staring at her as if mesmerized, which made Cora blush.

"Forgive me, I meant no ill will—"

"Say it again, Cora... what you just called me." He had drawn closer, and it dawned on her what he meant.

"Husband." She had spoken in no more than a whisper, while Gavin came closer still.

"Is this a dream, wife? If so, I dinna ever wish tae wake."

She shook her head slowly, her breath caught at how he looked at her. His gaze swept her from head to toe as if he wanted to remember for all time how she was dressed as his bride.

"You're so beautiful, Cora."

So close now that he reached out to rub the lacy edge of her veil between his fingers, she felt a shiver course through her even though he hadn't touched her.

Her color must have heightened for he stepped back at once, and looked concerned as he searched her face.

"I didna mean tae cause you any unease—"

"You didna, truly. I... I want you tae touch me."

She heard his breath catch and he stared at her as if he didn't quite believe what she had said, which made Cora rush on.

"Do you remember telling me that one day I willna think of the past for it will have all washed away? We were standing together under the stars—"

"Aye, I remember."

His voice had grown husky, his darkened eyes holding hers as Cora could not help thinking how beautiful he was to her, too.

So broad-shouldered and masculine, a flicker of desire igniting within her. Only Gavin had ever made her feel this way... her true love.

"Help me wash away the past, husband... tonight, tomorrow, every day we have together, I beg you—"

"Och, woman, you dinna have tae beg me tae hold you, kiss you..."

He said no more, but drew Cora into his arms to look down into her face, one hand reaching up to caress her neck, her cheek.

His touch was so tender, making her feel as if she was melting against him as his lips found hers.

His kiss gentle at first, almost featherlight, but

deepening as she gasped beneath the pressure of his mouth and parted her lips to him.

His tongue found hers, his kiss grown deeper still and so ardent now that she leaned into him, wanting more... *needing* more.

Her arms flew around his neck to draw him closer as they stood there together, lost to the wonder that the heavens had bestowed upon them.

They were finally alone together, husband and wife!

Cora felt moisture well beneath her eyelids at so miraculous a blessing, and she heard a low groan from Gavin as if he shared the same thought.

Then he was stepping away from her to draw her to the side of the bed, Cora half stumbling, she felt so dazed from his kiss.

Yet she truly felt dizzy when he pulled her close to kiss her again, even more impassioned this time, but so briefly that she was startled when she opened her eyes to see him lifting the veil from her head.

"You willna be needing this... or this..."

He had tossed the veil onto a chair and gathered her silvery gown at her hips to draw it easily over her head. Cora sucked in her breath as she stood before him in nothing more than a delicate linen shift.

The room was warm, a fire blazing brightly in the fireplace, but she shivered, which made him sweep her into his arms to lay her upon the bed.

Then he was gone from her, but for no more than a few moments as he made as short work of his clothing as he had done to hers—Gavin soon standing naked in front of her.

She had already thought him beautiful, but nothing could have prepared her for the muscular magnificence of his body limned in firelight.

She could but stare at him in wonder, from his dark red hair that appeared tinged with flame, brushing his shoulders, to the powerful breadth of his chest tapering to lean hips and long, strong legs—ah, God, but it was the way *he* looked at her that made her tremble.

With desire, aye, but with such love as he joined her on the bed, the mattress dipping beneath his weight, and lay down beside her.

"I've longed for this moment... yet feared it might never happen..."

His voice seemed to catch, Cora touched more deeply than she could say by so vulnerable an admission from so formidable a man, which made her reach up to cradle his face.

"I love you, Gavin MacLachlan. Never forget how much..."

She felt him trembling now, too, moisture glimmering in his eyes as he bent his head to kiss her for so wondrous a few moments, Cora was breathless when he drew back from her.

Not to release her, but to slip his hand beneath her shift to pull it with a tearing sound from her body... now laid bare before him.

His gaze lingered over her, making her shiver all the more, but it was his sudden intake of breath and low curse that made her freeze upon the bed.

"Gavin?"

She knew before he had uttered a word that he saw the pink teeth marks on her left hip, and another similar scar along the curve of her right breast, his hand shaking as he traced them with his finger.

"Seoras did this tae you—"

"Aye, but I dinna want tae think of him ever again! Let us never speak of him again—promise me!"

Her voice grown hoarse, Cora feared from Gavin's hardened expression that he might not be able to heed her—mayhap ever—until he rose abruptly onto his knees to straddle her, his eyes burning into hers.

"Forgive me, my love. I swear tae you that I will never again say his name."

She nodded at him, her throat so tight she couldn't speak, tears filling her eyes.

Yet if she had thought he lowered his head to kiss her mouth, a sigh of surprise burst from her when he bent low to first kiss the scar upon her hip... and then the one at her breast.

His lips pressing fervently as if he could erase them from her skin, though in Cora's heart, he had done so.

She felt a tear trickle down her cheek when he trailed a soft line of kisses to her nipple... and then conscious thought fled.

The warmth of his mouth upon her like nothing she could have ever dreamed, Gavin flicking at her with his tongue and suckling her by turns, making Cora writhe beneath him.

His heated kisses and caresses suddenly seemed everywhere upon her body so that her head spun, such desire flaring inside her that she felt afire from her head to her toes.

She heard him groan and felt him trembling as if he was seized by the same driving need to banish swiftly whatever had come before to leave only her and Gavin—*ah, God!* Cora opened herself to him as he pushed apart her legs with his knees and buried himself inside her.

Her arms wrapping around his back, her splayed fingers digging into his skin. She met his quickening thrusts with equal fervor, lifting her hips to him to take in more of him—all of him.

His mouth covering hers at the same moment she cried out his name... his impassioned kiss silencing what would have been a scream of release that shook her to the depths of her being.

Her legs locked around him as his body throbbed its own release in a hot rush at the very heart of her.

All the longing, all the hope culminating in one blinding moment that left her limp beneath him... her face damp with tears, his cheek pressed to hers, his ragged breathing fanning her as their bodies lay locked together.

The past gone... their future bright before them, Cora whispering a prayer of thanks some moments later as Gavin raised himself on his elbows to look down at her.

His tender, aye, and somewhat sheepish smile, endearing him more deeply into her heart.

"Och, lass, it seems I possess no restraint at all when it comes tae you."

"Nor I for you, husband," she teased him, a shiver coursing through her at the rekindling desire she saw reflected in his eyes. "A good thing we're so well-matched, aye?"

She felt his low chuckling against her belly, but it was the pressing of his hips to hers that made her gasp and throw her arms around his neck to hold him tight.

A soft giggle escaping her as she felt his body swelling inside hers, which made her move her hips against him—and now it was Gavin who teased her lustily as he bent his head to kiss her.

"Well-matched, indeed, wife."

GAVIN AWOKE with a start to a stirring scene that he had dreamed a thousand times—only now become real.

Cora asleep beneath his arm, her tousled head nestled against his chest. Her slow, steady breathing like the softest whisper across his skin, making him loathe to move a muscle so as not to wake her.

He wanted this moment never to end.

His wife snuggled against him after much of the night spent loving each other, kissing each other, holding each other. . . until through the window of their bedchamber, the dawn streaking the sky in hues of purple and orange had found them succumbing to sweet exhaustion.

Now it appeared midmorning from the brightness of the day, which was much later than Gavin ever slept —but it had been their wedding night, after all.

Their wedding night. . .

Such contentment and peace washed over Gavin that he could have fallen asleep again if only to prolong their time together. He could hear the morning's commotion drifting to them from the bailey, horses whinnying and people talking with each other, punctuated by masculine bursts of laughter.

Gavin smiled wryly. Mayhap those were some of the clansmen who had so riotously accompanied him and Cora to their bedchamber last night—God help him, the muscles in his arms felt sore after preventing them from shoving their way into the room.

The memory of the laughter he had shared with Cora made him chuckle, though he fell silent when she stirred in his arms. . . but only to stretch a little and then sigh softly.

Gavin groaned to himself and focused upon the

brocade canopy overhead, for even that small movement had been enough to rouse him.

His lower body grown thick and hard, which should have astounded him after the night he had shared with Cora... but he would never feel sated with her.

The smell of damask roses—the vial of perfume a gift from Magdalene—melded with the warmth of Cora's natural scent, was intoxicating to him.

He groaned again, the bulge underneath the covers proof that his body was rebelling against his intent to lie still so she could sleep longer, but there didn't appear to be anything he could do about it. Och, other than waking her and dealing with his current state in the most tempting way he could imagine—

"Blast and damn, *what...*?"

A vigorous knocking upon the door made Gavin utter another curse as Cora fluttered open her eyes, startled awake beside him.

He could do nothing more than utter a few soothing words to her before throwing back the covers and lunging from the bed to cross the room.

He didn't care in the least that he stood naked as he unbolted the door and threw it open. A clansman stepped back in surprise while a young maidservant behind him, carrying a tray laden with breakfast, gasped aloud.

"F-forgive me, Baron, but Earl Gabriel has summoned you tae the great hall. King Robert and his forces are soon tae continue deeper into the Highlands and he wishes tae meet with his commanders before they set out."

Gavin nodded without a word. Truly, a request from the king was the *only* thing that would steal him from Cora's side the morning after their wedding.

He gestured for the maidservant to enter the room, the young woman blushing to her scalp as she deposited the tray upon a table and then hastily exited.

Gavin had already gone to where he had dropped his clothing onto the floor the night before and pulled his tunic over his head, his gaze meeting Cora's.

"I heard," she murmured, looking as disappointed as Gavin felt as he tied the plaid breacan around his waist and draped one end over his left shoulder. "Will you return tae me soon?"

The longing in her voice was enough to make him stride to the bed to lean over her and kiss her soundly. "Aye, wife, I'll not be leaving you for long."

She looked so beautiful with her black hair spread upon the pillow, her eyes as blue as the deep ocean and filled with such love.

For him.

He kissed her again, her lips so soft and warm, which made it all the harder for him to leave her, the clansman waiting for him just outside the room.

The man stepped back at the scowl Gavin threw him as he shut the door firmly behind him.

"Aye, Baron, I dinna blame you. . . leaving your bonny bride, but it's the king. . ."

Gavin didn't utter anything but a muted curse and strode down the hall, the clansman rushing after him.

Chapter 21

"I understand, my lord king. Cora and I will leave for our new home this very day."

Gavin watched as King Robert nodded his approval, everyone looking somber around the large table where they sat: Gabriel, Cameron, Conall, Finlay, and Rory, along with some of the king's captains. A striking contrast after the merriment of last night's wedding feast, but it was a time of war, after all.

"Aye, MacLachlan, I regret tae say the festivities are at an end. My men and I march north tae lay siege tae castles held by the English and their Scots vassals while all of you remain in Argyll to ensure the Mac-Dougalls dinna rally. We canna allow that traitorous clan tae regain any ground."

A solemn "Aye," came from every Highland warrior present, Gabriel's the loudest. As earl, he was commander of the region with only King Robert above him, his expression as resolute as he had sounded.

"We willna fail you, my lord king."

"Good." His light brown eyes as serious, the king turned back to Gavin. "I wasna pleased tae hear of the loss of your ship—a fine vessel. Yet that red sail marked you as a target tae our enemies, so it's best you command a birlinn like all the others. By now three more ships are heading for Castle MacLachlan tae enlarge your fleet, and your ships here are being loaded with supplies so they'll soon be ready tae sail."

Castle MacLachlan.

Gavin couldn't deny that hearing his name associated with the estate the king had awarded him filled him with pride, though he felt a bit of embarrassment, too, that he had been abed while so much had already been done.

"Och, man, you didna think we'd drag you from your lovely bride at dawn, now did you?"

Laughter flew around the table at Gabriel's comment, a moment of levity soon over as King Robert once more leveled his gaze upon Gavin.

"The raider who attacked your ship must be captured and hung—and all of his crew with him. I willna have Ranulf MacDougall plaguing my fleet any longer, nor any raiders that think my ships—now *your* ships—are fair game for plunder. If they keep tae English or French vessels, I've no quarrel with them, but otherwise—"

"I'll burn their ships tae ashes upon the sea."

Gavin had spoken with such grim resolve that King Robert didn't seem to have anything more to say on the matter, and rose from the table, everyone standing up with him.

"God be with all of you—and God save Scotland."

"God save Scotland!" came the resounding response.

All of the men walked from the great hall with the king and his captains, and while everyone headed toward the arched doorway leading to the bailey, Gavin turned toward the tower.

His mind already on Cora, his plan to tell her about the king's order for them to leave, and then rejoin the others—

"Magdalene will see tae her, man," came Gabriel's voice to draw him back, though his eyes held a glint of understanding. "We've still much tae do before you sail."

"Aye," Gavin murmured, tamping down the image in his mind of Cora waiting for him as he followed Gabriel out the door.

∽

"I CANNA BELIEVE you must leave us so soon," Magdalene lamented to Cora as they stood together on the grassy shoreline, a brisk wind whipping at their hair.

With the last of the supplies loaded upon the

ships, Cora knew Magdalene and Gabriel had done everything they could to ensure she would have what she needed to set up a household at Castle MacLachlan. They were even sending along some servants until she could enlist her own from the nearby village.

It seemed every possible necessity had been touched upon: foodstuffs, bedding, more fabric, on and on, the cargo wells in the two birlinns filled to bursting. She doubted there would be any room at all for her or the servants to seek shelter on the lead ship if a storm broke. The beautiful morning that had dawned so clear had become a cloudy afternoon portending rain, aye, she could smell it in the air.

"Och, Cora, I will miss you so!"

Magdalene threw her arms around her to hug her, their goodbye the hardest one of all.

Cora had already bid farewell to her parents, who had set out toward home with Rory... no longer an enemy but a staunch ally. Thankfully Blair Campbell's wound hadn't threatened the use of his arm, his gratitude to Gavin for sparing his life as heartfelt as his vow never to call him "Trout" again.

She had said goodbye to Keira and Rhona, too, though the girls had begged to accompany them to the loch. Their disappointment had been keen at Magdalene's firm refusal, the threat of a storm keeping them with their nursemaid. Only Cora's promise to have them come and visit her had brought smiles to their faces—och, she missed already their sweet hugs and kisses.

Cameron, Aislinn, and Sorcha would be returning home tomorrow, as well as Conall, Lisette, and Colin, and Cora wished she'd had more time to spend with her cousins and their families. Thankfully none of them were more than a few hours' journey from each other, which cheered her. Mayhap they could all gather soon at her and Gavin's new home, which made her hug Magdalene more tightly.

"I will miss you, too, Maggie—aye, so much. If not for you, I dinna know if Gavin and I would ever have—"

"Of course you would have found your way tae each other's arms!" Magdalene drew back to smile at her. "I'm so happy you were wed here. Every time I pray in the chapel, I will remember how beautiful you looked and how Gavin stared at you. I've never seen a man so in love—well, other than my Gabriel."

Her bright laughter made Cora smile in spite of the impending departure, and she glanced at the ships to see Gavin striding along the deck of the lead ship.

He looked so in command, his orders carrying upon the wind and immediately followed by crewmen scrambling to obey him. Yet even as he oversaw final preparations before they sailed, he took a moment to glance at her with a broad smile that made her heart skip a beat.

Her handsome raider—och, a raider no more, but the trusted commander of King Robert's fleet that would soon protect the western coast of Scotland. Cora felt such overwhelming pride, but a twinge of sadness, too, at the time they would spend apart, though she knew that was the life she had embraced as a warrior's wife.

"Aye, it will be hard tae be without your husband," Magdalene said as if reading her mind, compassion in her eyes. "Lonely, too, until you have bairns. I have Rhona and Keira, and by spring"—her hand fell to the soft rounding of her stomach—"this wee one. That's why you must love each other fiercely when you're together... with every breath—"

"Every kiss, every embrace," Cora finished for her, drawing Magdalene close to hug her again. "Thank you, my dearest friend."

Cora was almost grateful for the wind that had grown stronger, her tears whisked away as she squeezed Magdalene's hand and then hastened to where Gavin had jumped onto shore and stood waiting for her.

He drew her into his arms to hug her, and kissed her, too.

"Och, you're a vision in blue," he said against her ear, nuzzling her there before hoisting her easily over the railing, Brody waiting to assist her.

"Welcome aboard, Lady MacLachlan!"

The darkening sky seemed to enliven the helmsman, who cackled with laughter as he walked her over to where a canvas had been erected halfway between the mast and the stern.

"Not as snug as the cargo well, but it will keep you dry if it rains," he offered, before leaving her to take his place at the helm.

Gavin had climbed back aboard to join Brody in the stern, where he shouted out commands as their lead ship, and then the second birlinn, were shoved away from the shoreline and the oars lowered.

With a last glance at Magdalene, who stood within the shelter of Gabriel's arm, Cora ducked under the canvas, which was where she knew Gavin wanted her to be. Three maidservants were already huddled there and she greeted them, drawing her cloak more tightly around her.

"I've never been aboard a ship before!" cried the youngest one, from the look of her, her plump face flushed with worry.

"Aye, and it's soon tae storm," wailed another as

the wind whistled through the canvas. "I dinna want tae drown!"

Cora gave a laugh to calm them and reached out to clasp their hands, while the third maidservant, an older woman, didn't appear flustered at all.

"Och, it's just a wee bit of wind tae fill the sail, aye, Lady MacLachlan?"

She nodded, feeling a little uncertain herself after the last storm she had experienced, though she would never show it.

"Aye, a wee bit of wind. . ."

"We're almost tae the sea!" Brody shouted to Gavin, who squinted against the rain stinging his face and surveyed where the waters of the loch merged with the ocean in an angry swirl of currents.

At any other time than during a storm, their journey would not have been so rough, but the birlinn reared up and then dipped through the waves like a wild creature. Gavin braced his feet upon the rain-slicked deck and peered now to the southeast, which would be their new course as soon as they sailed from the loch.

Castle MacLachlan was only five leagues away, and he had thought they would reach their destination by nightfall. Now he wasn't so sure, the lead ship forging ahead in spite of the rocky waves, but the second vessel was lagging behind.

No doubt because of the furnishings Magdalene had insisted be loaded upon the deck, an intricately carved bed, an armoire, table, chairs—och, he could have declined her generous offer for the added weight to the ship, but Cora had looked so pleased.

In truth, Gavin had no idea what they would find once they reached the castle, though the king had said it was in good repair. Why not have Cora surrounded by fine things that Gabriel and Magdalene were so eager to share with them?

Gavin sighed heavily as he glanced behind them at the second birlinn dipping heavily as well through the waves. He would just have to wait upon that crew to catch up, since he didn't want the distance between them growing too great—

"Laird, a ship off tae starboard!"

Gavin swore under his breath at the tension in Brody's voice, for they both had been watching keenly for any sign of Ranulf.

He had hoped the raider might have abandoned his quest to track Gavin down after burning his ship—och, was it him? The rain was coming down so hard that the surface of the ocean seemed to boil, the loch now behind them, but Gavin still couldn't tell for sure—

"God help us, will you look at the devil?" Brody cried, spitting out rainwater. "He looks as if he intends tae ram us!"

Gavin couldn't believe it, either, but it was true—and now he saw the pitch-black flag atop the mast, damn Ranulf MacDougall to hell!

The raider's ship plunging through the waves and aimed directly at the center of Gavin's ship, where the canvas whipped in the wind, Cora huddled beneath it.

His heart pounding in his throat, Gavin lunged for the canvas as Ranulf's ship forged closer... closer...

"*Cora!* By God, get out! *Get out!*"

By some miracle she heard him above the whistling wind and rain, not only her, but three maidservants scrambling out from beneath the canvas as

Gavin shouted to Brody, "Hard tae port, man! *Hard tae port!*"

The ship seemed to groan from the sudden change of direction, and listed so dangerously that Gavin feared for a moment they might go over—

"*Gavin!*"

Cora's piercing scream chilled his blood. He reached out to grab her but caught only her cloak as she tumbled overboard with one of the maidservants —the other two shrieking in terror.

Gavin stood there in shock, staring at the two bobbing heads in the water that were already well beyond any reaching them from the ship.

"*Hard about, Brody!*"

Now the ship listed to starboard as his men pulled on their oars with all their might, the sea fighting them even as Ranulf's birlinn had slowed its advance and gone hard to starboard, too.

With a sickening realization, Gavin knew exactly what the raider was doing and there was no way to stop it, even when he turned his own vessel around.

He could see Ranulf's men hauling in a brace of oars on one side of the ship and then several of them leaned far over the railing, other crewmen holding them by the legs so they wouldn't fall into the sea.

Like a nightmare, he saw them dragging in first the maidservant in her white apron and then Cora in her gown of light blue—Gavin roaring at his men to row faster, though his clenched gut told him they wouldn't catch up with Ranulf's ship in time.

Gavin's unspeakable relief that Cora had been retrieved from the sea was overcome by fury that Ranulf had her now. He could see the huge raider staring across the boiling surf and laughing at him—by God, *laughing!*

Gavin ran back to the stern, Brody's face stricken and his knuckles white as he gripped the helm.

No words had to be spoken between them, Gavin pounding his fists upon the railing as Brody steered their ship hard into the wind to surge after them.

Ranulf's birlinn already heading straight out to sea —with Cora.

19

Dripping wet and shivering to the bone, Cora lowered her head as Ranulf MacDougall bellowed with laughter. She had recognized him at once—though he seemed not to have recognized her.

Or so she thought until a huge hand lifted her chin to face him, the swarthy brute of a man staring down at her in surprise.

"Lady Cora? What folly is this? How came you tae be aboard MacLachlan's ship?"

She stared up at him in surprise, too, as the young maidservant huddled on the deck beside her, her plump face ashen, coughed and sputtered up seawater.

Ranulf didn't know that she was Gavin's wife! Yet how could he? She was determined to keep it that way, her mind racing as he lifted her to her feet as if she weighed nothing at all.

"Speak tae me, woman! It's a strange thing and I would know the meaning of it. We saw two lasses fall into the sea—aye, harlots, I judged, but *you*? After Seoras was slain, I heard you had gone north and taken refuge with your clan."

"A-aye, so I d-did!" Cora blurted, her teeth chattering so badly it was hard for her to talk. "I-I was visiting my former sister-in-law at M-MacLachlan Castle. The baron was returning me tae my parents—"

"*Baron*, you say?" Now Ranulf looked at her with suspicion, Cora realizing she had revealed too much. Her apprehension mounting that he would use her against Gavin if he knew the truth, she stumbled to answer.

"So he calls himself, I dinna know why—"

"Hellfire, woman, do you think me addled in the head that I canna guess what's afoot here?"

With that, Ranulf grabbed the sopping maidservant and hauled her roughly to her feet, a knife wrested from his belt and pressed to her throat.

"If you wish tae see this one's blood splashed upon the deck, tell me more lies. What are you tae that red-haired whelp who dares tae claim himself the devil of the seas? *I'm* as close to Satan as you'll ever meet in this world and you will answer me!"

Cora had never known such raw fear as she stared into Ranulf's enraged face, and she could barely utter above a whisper, "I-I'm his wife."

A flicker of astonishment lit the raider's dark eyes, but then he threw back his head and roared in triumph.

"No wonder he sails after us. Look!"

He dropped the maidservant, the poor girl crumbling with a whimper back onto the deck, and whirled Cora around like a puppet to face the stern.

"You see? I have the bastard right where I want him. He races after *you*, Lady MacLachlan, and when we reach the island, I'll finally have the gold. *My* gold."

He spoke now with such venom that Cora might

have crumpled to the deck herself if he had released her.

Yet Ranulf didn't let her go, but hoisted her up and settled her under his arm as if she were a sack of oat flour, and carried her toward a width of canvas erected near the mast.

She smelled him then, the rank odor of his body—in spite of the soaking rain—enough to make her gag.

If she had hoped the shelter would offer her some relief from the stench, she was sorely mistaken when he threw back the flap. The pallet upon the floor heaped with filthy blankets smelled just like him—and she realized this must be where he slept.

His crew left to fend for themselves out on the deck, the space only large enough for him and mayhap one other.

His coarse laughter chilled her as he thrust her inside the shelter and dropped her onto the pallet, but he didn't follow her inside.

"A few hours and we'll reach the island—dinna fear, woman, I'll not trouble you now. We will have plenty of time tae become much better acquainted after your husband leads me tae the gold... and you're made a widow once again. Mayhap I'll take a bonny bride myself."

Ranulf erupted in laughter again as he dropped the canvas flap to leave Cora in semidarkness, but she scrambled toward the opening in spite of the horror gripping her.

"My maidservant, please! Allow her tae join me—"

"What maidservant? She's gone. Thrown herself overboard before my men could greet her properly—and they're not too pleased about it."

"Oh, God..." Cora shook her head in disbelief as Ranulf's heavy footfalls moved away.

His blustered command to his men to row harder, faster, making her curl into a shivering ball, the flap cracked just enough to emit fresh air so she could breathe.

~

"The island is dead ahead, Laird. What is your plan?"

Plan? Gavin stared grimly at Brody while his exhausted crew took a few moments' break from rowing, the wind still gusting enough to propel the ship forward.

He had no plan—other than to do whatever he could to save Cora. He cared nothing for himself, only her.

Only her.

"We'll anchor in the harbor and the lot of you will stay aboard ship."

"Laird, I dinna think—"

"No arguments, Brody. I dinna know what will happen, but somehow I'll get her back tae you. You must be ready tae pull up anchor and row like hell tae save yourselves—tae save her."

Brody's hand a clenched fist upon the helm, Gavin could tell that the man didn't like what he had proposed, but that was all he had to offer.

With Cora as his prisoner, Ranulf could demand anything he wanted by threatening her life, which Gavin was certain the raider would do.

All for two chests of gold. Gavin clenched his fists as well in impotent fury.

He hated any semblance of feeling helpless, a useless emotion he allowed himself for only a moment before thrusting it away.

He wasn't helpless. He had more than enough hatred to fuel him, especially when he had seen the maidservant's lifeless body floating upon the waves.

In the distance he had seen her clamber in desperation over the railing and hurl herself into the sea, Ranulf's crew like slavering dogs attempting in vain to retrieve her.

The poor lass had drowned before Gavin's ship could reach her, and he had left her to sink into the depths.

His prayer for her soul followed by one of vengeance against Ranulf and his crew—aye, he would make them pay for her death as well as anything Cora might suffer. God help him, he couldn't bear to think of that stinking giant laying a finger upon her—

"They're signaling tae us, Laird. I believe Ranulf wants us tae follow them tae shore."

So they were signaling, one of MacDougall's crew waving a blazing torch as their ship sailed into the protected harbor and made straight for the rocky beach.

Other crewmen were scrambling to stow oars and furl their sail, Ranulf clearly so confident in Gavin obeying him that they weren't even bothering to drop anchor, which would have allowed them a faster departure than shoving their beached ship back into the water.

So much for his plan to anchor his birlinn out in the harbor as well. Gavin glanced at Brody, who looked pleased from this turn of events, as if eager for a fight.

"Aye, then, follow them in."

Gavin shouldn't have been surprised as Brody erupted into cackling laughter, knowing his pugnacious spirit, but it jarred upon him nonetheless as the helmsman steered the ship straight for the shore.

His own men hauling in and securing their oars, and then jumping up from their benches to furl the sail and prepare for beaching.

Gavin clenched his jaw as the bottom of the hull scraped along the pebbly rocks and slid to a grating stop, his gaze narrowed against the late afternoon sun that had broken through the clouds.

The rain had ceased an hour ago, though the wind had held steady, but that was subsiding now, too.

The calmer weather in stark contrast to the tempest churning inside Gavin as he searched Ranulf's deck for any sign of Cora, the raider's ship beached no more than thirty feet away.

Gavin didn't see her, which made his chest tighten and his breathing slow as an unsettling apprehension filled him—

"Och, Laird, there's your lady."

Brody had held his breath, too, but now his hand went to the hilt of the knife he always carried in his belt while Gavin's went to his sword.

Cora stared at him across the water rippling between the two beached ships, her face pale, her hair and gown still appearing damp, and he could see that she shivered.

Yet it was the slow shake of her head in warning that made Gavin move his hand away from his sword, Ranulf grabbing her roughly to shove her against the railing.

"You see your wife lives, MacLachlan—and if you wish her tae remain that way, you'll do exactly as I tell you. Dinna doubt that I will cut her throat if you or your crew dare tae defy me. Remove your sword belt and meet me on shore—aye, none of your men, just you."

Brody's sharp intake of frustration matched Gavin's own, but there was nothing to be done about it. Not yet... not yet.

He grimly obliged the raider, a few moments more finding him upon the beach surrounded by a half dozen armed crewmen and Ranulf himself... a towering hulk of a man who bore a fetid stench he seemed to revel in.

His grin mocking, Ranulf broke wind noisily as if he intended it as some sort of vile greeting for Gavin, who was grateful at least to see that Cora remained aboard the raider's ship.

"So at last we meet," grated Ranulf, sliding his gaze to Cora as well and laughing coarsely. "Aye, she's lovely. I used tae envy Seoras his wife... wishing it was me plowing her at night, and now look what heaven has bestowed upon me—"

"More the devil at work here," Gavin cut him off, not missing that Ranulf's dark eyes had narrowed at him, though the raider flashed a tight grin.

"Spew away, MacLachlan, your words mean nothing tae me. When we're done here today, I'll possess your treasure and your woman—and where will you be? Your corpse and those of your men floating upon the waves, your ship a bonfire, and Cora naked in my bed—aagh!"

Gavin had smashed his fist into Ranulf's face before it even registered what he had done, fury overwhelming his reason.

An instant later, he was driven to his knees by a fierce blow that made his eyes blur, the raider's own fist the size of three men's and with as much muscle behind it.

"Ha! Is this how it's going tae be?" roared Ranulf, hauling back and kicking Gavin in the gut.

He doubled over, the breath knocked from him, his abdomen on fire as he was hoisted to his feet. A second blow from the raider, this time to Gavin's jaw, made him spit out blood.

His arms pinned behind his back, there was nothing he could do to fight the man—and there was nothing his crew and Brody, who watched helplessly, could do, either. Not yet... not yet.

"Lead me tae the gold—*now*!"

Half stumbling and his head pounding from the two vicious blows, Gavin was forced to oblige Ranulf, one of the chests hidden in a cave at the far end of the beach.

With the pebbles shifting beneath his feet, he could feel Cora's stricken gaze burning into his back as Ranulf and his men shoved him along—Gavin wondering when, or if, he would be able to make a move before they had all of the gold in their possession and began the cold-blooded slaughter.

Gavin. His crew. God have mercy on them all, was there no miracle left for him and Cora?

~

"PLEASE, I NEED WATER." Cora's throat parched, she glanced at the dark-haired crewman who held a knife to her ribs, but he appeared unmoved by her plea and grunted a refusal.

They hadn't strayed at all from the railing where Ranulf had left her flanked by two of his men, both of them so burly that she wouldn't have a chance at struggling against them.

Cruel-looking, too, the raider's entire crew a fearsome lot from what she could see of them when she had dared to glance to her right and left.

All of them silent and staring at Gavin's ship beached only thirty feet away, as if watching for any of his crew to make a move—but Brody and the rest of Gavin's men stood silently as well, staring back.

An eerie standoff as they waited for Ranulf and Gavin to return from what appeared a steep cluster of rocks at one end of the beach—ah, God, she prayed her beloved husband would return!

She remembered Gavin had told her shortly after he executed his crewman that he had gold hidden on the island, but not where, and they had never since discussed it. How could they when their wedding had only been yesterday? They had so much yet to talk about. . . their hopes and dreams and the daily happenings of their lives—

"Stand still, woman!"

Cora gasped at how roughly one of her captors wrenched her arm, but she was shaking and could not seem to stop.

Just thinking that she may never see Gavin again was too much for her, her legs feeling so wobbly that she feared she might collapse.

"I-I'm trying. Please. . . if I could have some water. . ."

"Aye, we'd best get her a drink," spoke up the man standing on the opposite side of her. "Ranulf willna be pleased if she sickens."

"Hold her, then!" commanded her captor with the knife, the man withdrawing his weapon and shoving her toward his companion.

Cora stumbled toward the man, her sudden sense of freedom reviving her enough to dodge him and scramble over the railing.

She heard the men cursing and felt one of them grab her, but her nails digging into his hand made him let go and she plummeted into the thigh-deep water.

Her feet touched bottom and she lurched wildly toward Gavin's ship even as she heard splashes behind her, her captors coming after her.

Until a bloodcurdling shriek came right behind her, one of the men that close to catching her—and then another scream, and another.

The whiz of what sounded like arrows just over her head as Brody shouted to her, urging her on. Cora stumbled twice, but hauled herself up in spite of her sodden gown tangling around her legs.

Her breathing ragged, salt water stinging her eyes as she held up her arms to those waiting for her and felt herself lifted to safety aboard Gavin's ship.

"Stay down, Lady Cora!" she heard Brody admonish her as she ducked her head, the sounds of battle raging all around.

She felt arms reaching out for her and she was dragged underneath the shelter of the canvas, the two maidservants tearfully hugging her close.

She wept with them, grieving for the one they had lost so cruelly... hoping desperately for a victory over Ranulf's men... and praying that Gavin would survive so brutal an enemy even as she felt the ship begin to move.

"Please come back tae me, my love... please come back..."

20

"Bastard, you hid the gold deep enough," Ranulf groused to Gavin, who blinked against the sweat in his eyes and cleared sand from the top of the chest.

The air was so steamy in the cave that it was hard to breathe... made even more difficult by the raider's smell that hung like a pall over them, Gavin wheezing from the stench.

"By God, man, do you never bathe?" he couldn't help demanding in frustration, the widened eyes of Ranulf's men in the lantern light telling him that he had voiced a query they never broached. The raider merely laughed and broke wind with such force that Gavin was certain the man had soiled himself, disgusting him even further.

He dug faster, wanting to be done with this chest and on to the second one, which was buried at the bottom of a cliff on the opposite side of the beach.

He could do nothing to fight Ranulf in this cave, the rock walls so close around them that there was barely enough room to move around.

Grunting, Gavin heaved one last time and the chest broke free of the sand encasing it, Ranulf so eager to possess the gold that he shoved him violently out of the way.

Gavin's right shoulder struck the wall, making him wince. The raider only laughed with derision as he hauled the chest from the hole as if it were filled with goose feathers, and not coins.

"That's one, now lead me tae the other!"

Ranulf's booming voice echoed the length of the cave as Gavin massaged his sore shoulder and set out behind the crewman carrying the lantern, while the rest of them followed. The cave was no taller than it was wide, but it was long, nearly forty feet before he made a narrow turn and saw light coming from the entrance.

It was then, too, that he heard sounds that made the hair prickle on the back of his neck—aye, fighting, screaming, and men dying.

Ranulf must have heard it, too, for Gavin felt the sharp tip of a sword at his back before he had a chance to shove aside the crewman in front of him and bolt toward the entrance.

Cursing himself for not moving quicker, he could only grit his teeth and wonder what had happened, even as he prayed that his men were winning the battle and that Cora was safe.

Gavin dragged in great lungfuls of air as soon as he exited the cave, only to be felled by an unexpected blow from behind that dropped him to his knees.

Not a sword thrust, thankfully. He didn't need to glance behind him to know that Ranulf had struck him, the raider's vehement curses blistering the air.

"Hell and damnation, get him up!"

Gavin was hauled to his feet by two crewmen that cursed at him as well, another brandishing his sword at Gavin's throat.

"Let me kill him now, Laird—"

"Fool, not until we find the other chest, then you can stick him a hundred times!"

Gavin stared at Ranulf, thinking that *he* must be the fool to hear the clamor of battle and show so little concern about it. If the raider's men triumphed, he would still have a ship with which to leave the island —but if Gavin's men had the upper hand...

A quick glance down the beach told him with a swamping sense of relief that his ship was easing back from the beach, which meant only one thing.

His men were victorious, with Brody heeding Gavin's plan to anchor in the harbor, and Cora had to be with him. His helmsman would never have left her behind—

"*Move*, MacLachlan!"

Ranulf had hoisted the chest onto his immense shoulder and pointed his sword at Gavin, an unsettling glint in the man's dark eyes that made him certain the raider must be half mad... or more. All he seemed to care about was the gold, and not that they could plainly see the bodies of his men strewn upon the beach and slumped over the railing of his ship.

"Your crewman are dead, MacDougall! Does that mean nothing tae you? How will you get the gold off the island if you have no one left tae man your ship?"

As if Gavin's intent to provoke him had roused him from some treasure-induced daze, Ranulf gave a feral growl and dropped the gold to thrust his sword at Gavin, barely missing him.

Yet the raider screamed in fury when he saw that the chest had cracked open on the rocks and spilled the coins in all directions.

Ranulf's men stared in astonishment, too, which was exactly what Gavin had hoped for.

He grabbed the sword from the nearest one and cut him down, and swung with all his might at two others to slay them before they could even lift their weapons.

That left three more and Ranulf, who had dropped to his knees to try and gather up the gold. His remaining men came after Gavin, attempting to surround him.

"Drop your swords and live," he grated to them, but the crewmen gave no heed to his offer of mercy and attacked him anyway, their weapons flashing in the waning sunlight.

Two swords clattered onto the rocks as Gavin struck down the crewmen, his own sword wet with their blood.

The last man ran back toward Ranulf as if to enlist his help, only to find himself skewered by the raider's sword, his lifeless body dropping at Ranulf's feet.

"Blasted coward."

Gavin stared at him in disbelief, stunned that the raider had so mercilessly struck down one of his own —yet should he be surprised? He had heard plenty about Ranulf's brutality upon the sea, the man clearly possessing no soul at all.

Now he looked as if he had fully regained his wits, and sliced the air with his sword as he left the gold behind and advanced upon Gavin, who kept walking backward to bring him closer to his ship.

Aye, closer to Cora. . . though he thrust her from his mind.

All he focused upon was Ranulf, who bellowed like a bull and lunged toward him,

three hundred pounds of enraged bone and muscle intent upon his death. Gavin dodged what would have been a lethal blow—the raider's sword striking the rocks with a resounding ring.

Again and again Ranulf rushed at him in wild-eyed fury. Gavin evaded each blow and propelled them further down the beach until they were almost upon the silent tomb that the raider's ship had become.

Gavin saw some of his men had fallen, too, which made him glance to where his ship was anchored some forty feet from shore.

It was then he saw Cora standing at the railing. Such relief flooded him that he was momentarily distracted and didn't see what he had thought a lifeless body, moving near his feet.

The bloodied hand of one of Ranulf's men grabbed him by the ankle to trip him, Gavin falling backward as Ranulf thundered toward him, roaring in triumph.

The raider's sword raised to strike as Cora's scream cut through the air, Gavin thrusting his sword upward to try and fend off a violent blow that he sensed was going to kill him.

It seemed in his mind everything slowed down... a strange peace filling him even as he saw Ranulf's sword seem to fly from his hand, the raider dropping to his knees and crashing down upon Gavin.

The breath expelled from his lungs to have such a crushing weight atop him, only to feel it gone within the next moment as someone rolled Ranulf's body off to one side.

Wholly stunned that he still lived and breathed, Gavin could but stare up at a thin-faced man dressed in the simple brown garb of a monk, an empty sling in his hand.

Only then did Gavin realize what had happened as

he looked over to see the hole a stone had made in the center of Ranulf's forehead, blood streaming from the wound.

Next to the lifeless raider, the crewman who had tripped Gavin, Ranulf's sword impaling him to the ground.

"Let me help you," murmured the monk, who appeared at least thirty years older than Gavin, if not more, though his grip was strong and sure while assisting Gavin to his feet.

He could hear shouts of elation from his ship, though still he stared with astonishment at his aged rescuer. The man wasn't looking at him, but at Ranulf, and he spat upon the corpse... and then made the sign of the Cross over him.

"He killed five of my brother monks and slaughtered all of our goats... and nearly dropped me from a cliff. He deserved tae die, though I will pray that God forgives me. Look, your ship is coming back for you."

Indeed it was, Gavin's crew driving their oars into the waves until the hull of the birlinn was once again scraping upon the pebbly rocks—Brody jumping overboard into knee-deep water and holding up his arms.

For Cora.

She slid from the railing and landed with a splash, both of them laughing as Brody released her so she could wade to shore.

Toward Gavin.

Her eyes shining and her face flushed with joy, Cora lifted her sodden gown and ran the last few feet to launch herself into his arms.

Her kisses covering his face, her arms flying around his neck to hug him fiercely like she would never let him go.

Gavin could not say how long they stood there holding each other. When he looked up from Cora to offer his thanks to the man who had saved his life, the monk was nowhere to be seen.

Only the trail of his footsteps through tall grasses leading up and over a hill gave away his path, the man already headed back to the leeward side of the island.

Indeed, Gavin was certain he had witnessed a miracle... but the greatest one of all was his beloved wife smiling in his arms.

CASTLE MACLACHLAN
One Year Later...

"Och, have you ever heard such a fine pair of lungs on a babe?"

Gavin didn't quite know what to say to the stout nursemaid. The sight of two bairns nestled against Cora, their fists pumping and their legs kicking, still left him speechless.

"I meant the lass, of course," added Agnes with a chuckle. "You'll have your hands full one day with that red-haired beauty, I'll swear tae it. Go on and pick up the lad, Baron, you'll not break him."

With Cora's smile of encouragement, Gavin obliged the older woman that had attended to the birth, and lifted his son into his arms. Though small, he felt strong and solid, the downy hair atop his head the same midnight as his mother's.

Gavin glanced up at his beautiful wife, who had given him the greatest gift he could have imagined—other than marrying him a year ago.

Twins. . . a ruddy-faced son and a bonny wee daughter.

Another miracle that had blessed their lives, starting with when he had first seen Cora at his fish stall, her laughter touching his heart, to this very day. . . his wife and bairns healthy and whole—aye, and loud!

As if not wanting his younger sister to best him, his son began to flail his arms and wail to the heavens, leaving Gavin unsure of what to do as Cora gave a soft laugh.

"Hand him back tae me, husband, I think I know how tae quiet them."

Gavin obliged her, staring in awe as she snuggled both babes against her, Agnes helping to guide them to where they began to suckle greedily.

Their tiny fists resting against the curve of Cora's breasts, their lusty cries faded into the sweetest sounds Gavin had ever heard.

"They're hungry," he murmured in surprise, which made the nursemaid cluck her tongue at him.

"Och, Baron, you've much tae learn about bairns. After all that work tae greet you and your lady, of course they want a fine meal. . . and soon, a long nap."

Gavin chuckled in agreement with her; it was true he had much to learn and he was eager for all of it.

He had the family he'd always wanted, a home with Cora that she had lovingly made comfortable for them, and more time than he could have hoped for to spend with her as the coastline had been quiet these past months—aye, so many blessings.

"What shall we name them?" Cora whispered, for indeed, the two had drifted asleep just as Agnes had said they would. Gavin felt his throat grow so tight at the wonder of new life that for a moment he couldn't answer, and he leaned down to tenderly kiss Cora.

Her lips were so soft and warm that he lingered there until he heard the nursemaid cluck her tongue again, which made him draw back with great reluctance to stare into Cora's smiling eyes.

"Well. . . Gabriel and Magdalene have Debora, after her beloved sister. Cameron and Aislinn have Graham, and Conall and Lisette, their wee Dylan. What names move your heart, my love?"

Gavin's voice hoarse with tenderness, it was all he could do not to lean over and kiss Cora again as she rested her cheek against the top of their sleeping son's head.

"Logan."

"Aye, a fine name," he murmured as she gently pressed her lips to their daughter's brow.

"Leana."

"Aye. . . Leana," Gavin echoed, never having felt such fierce love as he did at that moment for his precious family.

Now he did lean down to kiss Cora. . . no amount of clucking from Agnes this time going to wrest him from her.

ALSO BY MIRIAM WALKER

Romance from sweet to sensual and historical to contemporary, you're sure to find stories to love!

Warriors of the Highlands

My Highland Warrior

My Highland Protector

My Highland Captor

My Highland Raider

My Highland Champion

THE MAN OF MY DREAMS

Regency Historical Romance

Secrets of Midnight

My Runaway Heart

My Forbidden Duchess

Kissed At Twilight

My Fugitive Prince

THE O'BYRNE BRIDES

Irish Medieval Historical Romance

Wild Angel

Wild Roses

Wild Moonlight

On A Wild Winter's Night

CAPTIVE BRIDES

Medieval Historical Romance

Twin Passions

Captive Rose

The Pagan's Prize

DANGEROUS MASQUERADE
18th Century Historical Romance

The Brigand Bride

The Scandalous Bride

The Impostor Bride

ROMANTIC SUSPENSE

Operation Hero

INSPIRATIONAL ROMANTIC SUSPENSE

Operation Rescue

TO LOVE A BILLIONAIRE

Steamy Contemporary Romance with an Historical Romance Story within a Story

The Maiden and the Billionaire

The Governess and the Billionaire

The Pirate Queen and the Billionaire

The Highland Bride and the Billionaire

WALKER CREEK BRIDES
Sweet Western Historical Romance

Kari

Ingrid

Lily

Pearl

Sage

Anita

ABOUT THE AUTHOR

Miriam Minger is the bestselling author of sweet to sensual historical romance that sweeps you from Viking times to Regency England to the American West. Miriam is also the author of contemporary romance, romantic suspense, inspirational romance, and children's books. She is the winner of several Romantic Times Reviewer's Choice Awards—including Best Medieval Historical Romance of the Year for The Pagan's Prize—and a two-time RITA Award Finalist for The Brigand Bride and Captive Rose.

Miriam loves to create stories that make you live and breathe the adventure, laugh and cry, and that touch your heart.

For a complete listing of books as well as excerpts and news about upcoming releases, and to connect with Miriam:

<u>Visit Miriam's Website</u>
<u>Subscribe to Miriam's Newsletter</u>